Tom wandered over to the fireplace mantel, where a photograph of a smiling man in uniform held a place of honor

Alongside it was a wedding picture of a smiling bride and groom, as well as small snapshots of the twins as babies, held by their smiling father. Since there were no later pictures of the family together, he guessed that Paul Sr. had died soon after the twins' birth.

In spite of his earlier determination not to become emotionally involved with Lili, her past, present or future, Tom felt a tug at his heart.

So much for being all business.

ROMANCE

Dear Reader,

My three-book series SULLIVAN'S RULES features stories of three women who work for a magazine in Chicago, Illinois.

The first release, *Marriage in Six Easy Lessons* (AR #1023), was the story of April Morgan and Lucas Sullivan, the man who created six rules about what a woman must be to participate in the mating game. April, his editor, sets Lucas straight. To their surprise, the lessons lead to marriage.

The second book, *How To Marry the Boy Next Door* (AR #1048), was the story of Rita Rosales. Rita has her own ideas about love and marriage. Physical attraction aside, she feels that a man has to have strong genes to pass on to her children. To Rita's surprise, the man who qualifies is Texas Ranger Colby Callahan, the boy who lived next door in Texas.

This final book in the series, *An Engagement of Convenience,* is the story of Lili Soulé, a single mother and a graphic artist for the magazine. Taken with the editor, Tom Eldridge, Lili yearns for him to notice her. What she does to draw his attention motivates Tom to suggest an engagement of convenience so that he can keep an eye on Lili before she brings the magazine down around his ears.

I think there's a little of April, Rita and Lili in all of us.

Enjoy.

Mollie Molay

AN ENGAGEMENT OF CONVENIENCE
Mollie Molay

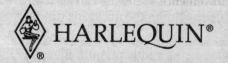

HARLEQUIN®

TORONTO • NEW YORK • LONDON
AMSTERDAM • PARIS • SYDNEY • HAMBURG
STOCKHOLM • ATHENS • TOKYO • MILAN • MADRID
PRAGUE • WARSAW • BUDAPEST • AUCKLAND

ISBN 0-373-75075-7

AN ENGAGEMENT OF CONVENIENCE

Copyright © 2005 by Mollie Molé.

www.eHarlequin.com

Printed in U.S.A.

To Child Care Centers everywhere
and to the loving and caring people who run them.

Books by Mollie Molay

HARLEQUIN AMERICAN ROMANCE

*Grooms in Uniform
†Sullivan's Rules

Don't miss any of our special offers. Write to us at the
following address for information on our newest releases.

Harlequin Reader Service
U.S.: 3010 Walden Ave., P.O. Box 1325, Buffalo, NY 14269
Canadian: P.O. Box 609, Fort Erie, Ont. L2A 5X3

Sullivan's Rules

1. A happy relationship requires that a woman make her man feel masculine.

2. While a man is not monogamous by nature, he is more likely to see a woman as a potential girlfriend or mate if sexual intimacy doesn't occur too soon.

3. A woman must rein in her own desires to promote the health of a relationship.

4. A woman must strive for compatibility, rather than try to be sexy.

5. A woman must show her man how much she likes and appreciates him. She must shower him with affection and sublimate her own daily frustrations.

6. A woman must be supportive, fun loving, easygoing and generous in her praise of a man's achievements.

Chapter One

"So, you're the one!"

At the sound of her boss's angry voice, Lili Soulé tried to cover the papers on her drafting table, but it was too late. The flier demanding that the management of the Riverview Building keep its child care center open was in full view—along with a charcoal sketch of Tom Eldridge, publisher of *Today's World* magazine and Lili's boss.

For a man who took great pains to avoid associating with employees, Eldridge sounded friendly enough at weekly staff meetings. But he sure didn't sound friendly now.

Lili's heart raced. She'd been working as a graphic artist at the magazine for two years, and her crush on the publisher was as strong as ever. Tom Eldridge was six feet of rugged masculinity, with a square jaw and chocolate-brown eyes—eyes that were unmistakably angry as he regarded the damning evidence. The frown that creased his forehead did nothing to calm her racing heart, but now that her identity as the child care center's staunchest advocate was out in the open, she intended to defend herself. She nodded cautiously.

"So you're the person who's been circulating fliers and a petition to keep the day care center open?" he asked.

Lili tried to hide her discomfort as she looked up at him. "Someone has to do it."

His scowl made her toes curl. "And that someone had to be you?"

Lili couldn't deny his accusation, not with the evidence right in front of her. The damage was done. Still, if ever there was a time to assert herself and her right to free speech, this was it. After all, she reminded herself, her cause was just.

"Yes. I have twins in the after-school program. Once I heard that Riverview's management might close the center, I felt I should do something before it was too late." Her defiant reply seemed to surprise both of them.

Raised in a small town in the south of France by grandparents who had taught her to treat everyone with respect no matter how she felt about them, Lili seldom raised her voice. Especially not around the office. Until today.

Eldridge's eyes narrowed. He pointed to the assignment sheet pinned to the corner of her drawing board. "With a family to support, I would have thought you'd be spending your time designing the magazine rather than causing trouble."

Lili swallowed hard. "Actually, I was working on the magazine, but other things got in the way."

"Yeah," he agreed, glancing down at the betraying evidence. "It sure looks as if they did, and they're causing problems for everyone, including me."

This time, Lili's heart plunged to her toes, but she didn't intend to back off. The center had provided day care for her children for the past two years. Now that the twins were in public school, she still needed after-school care. Besides, no matter how Eldridge felt about her underground activities, a lot of parents depended on her campaign. She wasn't in this just for herself.

"I heard that the building's management has called a meeting of the tenants in two weeks to vote on the center's closure," she said when she realized that if she didn't speak up, Eldridge might fire her. "I'm not the only parent in the building involved, but since I am the only artist, I felt it was up to me to create this flier."

"You might be an artist, but I'm sure you can still do the math, Lili," Eldridge said. "Anyone who reads the newspapers has to be aware that insurance liability rates have gone up every year and are still climbing. So are the wages for well-trained caretakers and everything else that goes into a quality day care center like ours."

At his use of the word *quality,* Lili perked up. At least Eldridge recognized the center's worth. "Yes," she agreed. "But for the employees, it is both more convenient and less expensive than hiring baby-sitters."

"Perhaps," he agreed, "but for tenants like this magazine, the costs of operating the center keep rising. I realize children's welfare is involved here, but to the management, business is business."

"I know," Lili agreed, wishing she weren't so distracted by the sound of Tom's voice, even when he was angry with her. "That is why the next thing I am going to do is start a fund-raising campaign." Too late, she realized that by advertising her future plans, she was adding fuel to a burning fire.

"You haven't heard a word I've said, have you?" Eldridge muttered grimly.

"But of course I have," she retorted. "It is just that we do not seem to agree."

"There's nothing personal in this, Lili." He gave a slight shrug. "I've been trying to tell you that while I understand the problem, I don't own the building. Any decision the management may come to will be based strictly on financial considerations."

Lili saw red. "Ensuring the proper care of an employee's children should be just as much a part of running a business as making a profit," she argued. "As long as the children are taken care of, absentee rates will stay down!"

Tom shook his head. "It's not only me, you know. Even if I sympathize with you, in the long run I don't matter. Some of the building's tenants are not too happy with those petitions and fliers you've been circulating. They've complained that employees are being distracted from their work. Riverview's management has no choice. The word is out to find and stop the culprit." He gestured to the drafting table. "The flier you're working on is only going to stir things up again." He turned to leave. "I'd advise you to tear it up and go back to work."

Lili impulsively reached out to stop him. His tense arm muscles told her he was still angry.

"Not if you help us to buy time. You can ask for a postponement of the meeting. That would give me time to find a way to keep the center open."

"I only have one vote, Lili," Eldridge said, glancing down at her hand. "What I think isn't worth much. Not in tight financial times like these. As I just said, from the management's viewpoint, business comes first."

"And from yours?"

Eldridge hesitated, then took a step closer to her drawing board. "I might sympathize with your problem, but I don't have a great deal of influence."

To Lili's dismay, he reached over, picked up the charcoal drawing she'd been working on and held it up to the light. "What's this supposed to be? A wall target for you to pitch darts at?"

That's not what Lili had intended when she'd started the sketch of his face. Rather, she'd been wistfully wondering what it would be like to kiss him.

That was ridiculous, she knew. After all, she was a mature woman, a single mother, not an infatuated teenager.

"No," she said softly. "I heard the sound of your voice and somehow started drawing your face...." It was not a very convincing explanation, but it would have to do.

Tom put the sketch back on the drawing board, reached for the piece of charcoal and filled in the eyebrows. "As long as you've gone this far, it might as well look more like me." He handed the drawing back to Lili and, in a voice that set the hair at the back of her neck tingling, warned, "Let's just say that if I were you, I'd stop causing any more trouble around the building. I'm willing to forget I found the flier this time, but I might not be able to the next."

Lili silently stared after Eldridge as he left the studio. Whatever fantasies she'd had about getting to know him on a personal level had just been destroyed. She turned back to her work. No matter what he said about not circulating petitions or handing out fliers, she was determined to find some way to keep the center open.

TOM MADE HIS WAY back to his office, wondering how he could have been so off the mark when it came to Lili Soulé. Could this be the same ethereal woman who had floated in and out of the art studio for the past two years? There obviously lurked a will of steel under that shy smile. Lili was the last person he would have expected to be the mastermind behind the fliers and petitions circulating through the buildings.

A red-blooded man, he couldn't help noticing Lili's sapphire-blue eyes and blond tousled hair whenever he wandered into the art studio or attended staff meetings. But that was where his interest ended. He had a Business Only policy when it came to his employees and he didn't intend to change now.

As far as delaying Riverview's monthly meeting or voting to keep the center open, hell, he was as sympathetic as the next guy, but it was his job to keep *Today's World* out of the red and his lease out of trouble.

Since it had been a dire complaint from the building's management that had brought him to the art studio this morning in the first place, he didn't know why he hadn't fired Lili on the spot when he'd discovered that flier. There was a clause in his lease that stated *Today's World*'s rental agreement could be canceled if an employee undertook any activity that could be construed as defaming management. Maybe it had been the scent of her perfume, or perhaps her quaint French accent that had distracted him. Either way, he was beginning to feel as if he'd been seeing Lili for the first time. And he had to admit he liked what he saw—a mixture of an old-fashioned woman and a tantalizing modern one.

Too bad she was off-limits.

The way Riverview's manager had put it, one-half of the business owners were in favor of closing the center. Another third were for keeping it open, and the rest appeared to be undecided. Lili obviously was out to get that minority on her side, and the process was turning Riverview's tenants into warring camps.

All things considered, he was actually proud of the way he'd kept his cool with Lili instead of firing her.

LILI HEADED STRAIGHT for a heart-to-heart with her close friends April Morgan Sullivan, one of the magazine's editors, and Rita Rosales Callahan, the magazine's research librarian, who had just returned from her honeymoon. Confessing her undercover activities and her disastrous meeting with Tom Eldridge might not be wise, Lili realized, but if she couldn't ask her two closest friends for advice, whom else could she appeal to?

Lili found the two women at the watercooler.

"No way!" Rita said when Lili finished telling the story of how Tom had caught her planning another flier and sketching his likeness!

Rita's dark eyes lit up with interest. "I know I advised you to try to get Tom's attention, but that sure was one heck of a way to go about it! What happened after he caught you?"

Lili shivered as she mentally revisited the scene in the art studio. "For a minute I thought he was angry enough about the flier to fire me. Instead, when he noticed the sketch of him I was making, something about him seemed to change."

Rita grinned. "What did he say?"

"Not much," Lili confessed, "although I knew he was still upset. For that matter, so was I." She frowned.

"Until today, whenever he visited the studio, I was sure he was trying to satisfy his artistic side."

"Tom, an artist? No way," Rita scoffed. "All the man seems interested in is the way the magazine's circulation is going through the roof after he published those rules of Lucas's."

Rita was right, Lili thought. Not that she blamed Tom. Lucas Sullivan was a sociologist and Tom's long-time friend. After his six recommendations to guarantee a happy marriage—Sullivan's Rules—were published in *Today's World,* the magazine sold more copies than in its entire history. But there had been an even more delightful result as well—Lucas had fallen in love and married Lili's friend April, his editor.

"I would love to have seen the expression on his face when he caught you working on another one of those fliers," April said.

"He didn't look happy. He warned me to stop, but not before he practically took the piece of charcoal out of my hand and filled in the eyebrows on my sketch."

"Get outta here!" Rita exclaimed. "I didn't think the man had a sense of humor. But if you really are interested in him, I hope you took the time to talk about something besides work."

"No." Lili doubted Tom had been interested in a personal conversation. "I'm afraid it was all business."

Rita tossed her empty paper cup into a wastebasket. "All this time I thought you wanted him to notice you…to get to know you."

"Well, he did notice me, but not in the way I would have wished," Lili admitted.

Rita threw up her hands. "I can't believe you wasted such a great opportunity to get personal. Now, if it had been me and I hadn't already met my Colby, I would have…" She stopped and grinned happily. "What happened then?"

"Not much. He told me I should stick to business during working hours."

"Well, I suppose any conversation is a start. Although I think you could at least have cracked a joke or two about having been caught."

"A joke?" Lili said doubtfully. "Mr. Eldridge is always so serious, I'm not sure he has a sense of humor."

"Sure he does." April broke in with a laugh. "He managed to bring Lucas and me together when I was Lucas's editor. Considering the way Lucas and I disagreed about those rules of his, only Tom could have thought the two of us belonged together."

Rita sniffed. "From what I've seen, Tom's a man without a romantic bone in his body. Just what is it that attracts you to him anyway, Lili?"

"Well, to begin with, his eyes." Lili smiled as she also remembered Tom's deep, husky voice—even if he had been telling her off. "I know neither of you thinks Mr. Eldridge is sexy, but I do."

"Ha!" Rita scoffed. "Don't get me wrong, Lili. I'm the first to respect Tom for the way he's brought the magazine's circulation around. But if the man's sexy, then I'm the tooth fairy."

April waved her hand in warning as other members of the staff began to drift back from lunch. "Don't worry, Lili. Knowing how decent a man Tom really is, I'm convinced he won't stay angry with you for long. If you want us to help, I'm sure we can figure out a way to keep the center open without causing a riot."

"I agree," Rita said airily. "I might need to use the center myself someday."

Lili gaped at her. "You are expecting a baby already?"

Unabashed, Rita grinned. "You might say I'm working on it." She turned to April. "What about you?"

April laughed and shook her head. "Not for a while. Lucas and I are busy researching a new slant on his old study about the mating game."

"It's about time," Rita said. "Anyone who believes in his rules about the subservient way a woman ought to behave toward a man in the twenty-first century should have their head examined. As for you, Lili, I actually think Tom has more 'Sullivan' traits in him than most men do. Maybe what he needs is someone like you to show him what women really want."

"Just look at Colby and you, Rita," April teased. "The poor man had to get himself shot before he realized he loves you just the way you are—the way you've been ever since you were kids back in Texas. Still—" April winked at Lili "—maybe it's too much to expect you to take Rita's advice about Tom."

"Sheesh," Rita grumbled. "I didn't tell her to…well, not exactly. I just told her to do something to try to get Tom's attention."

"Yeah, I remember that conversation," April said dryly. "But it's what you suggested Lili *do* that was the problem. No matter how you put it, your advice boiled down to sex, sex and more sex!"

Instead of denying April's accusation, Rita looked pleased with herself. "It was all talk, I swear, but the truth is," she added with a wicked grin, "making love with Colby instead of talking was what finally worked for me. You have to remember, Lili, you're never going to really get Tom's attention if you keep calling him Mr. Eldridge instead of just Tom, the way the rest of us do."

"I know," Lili said wistfully. "I find it difficult to be familiar with him without an invitation. After all, he *is* my boss."

"And he's all business when he's at work," Rita added. "If you're ever going to catch his interest, you'll have to spread a little honey instead of making fliers."

"Maybe the problem is that you actually believe in Sullivan's Rules, Lili," April interjected. "You've already told us you were brought up to believe that a woman's role in a relationship is actually a lot like Lucas's rules for marriage."

"It is true," Lili agreed. "The women in my family were taught from childhood to defer to their father, then their husband. I know it sounds very old-fashioned compared to the way women here in the United States think, but it is different in my country. Especially for a girl like myself, who was raised by her grandmother."

"Then you and Tom ought to get along just fine," Rita said soothingly. "I think he actually believes in Sullivan's Rules. Provided you get over your shyness, and if you can do something to get him to see you're a mixture of the woman in Lucas's article and today's woman, you'll be okay."

"Rita's right," April agreed. "All Tom needs is to realize you're almost as old-fashioned about men as he is about women." She paused to look critically at Lili. "Or *are* you really an old-fashioned woman? Sometimes when I see the look in your eyes, I think there are hidden depths within you."

Lili blushed as she recalled her physical reaction to Tom whenever he was near. "Maybe so."

"Yeah." Rita grinned. "Personally, I believe that most rules are made to be broken—including Sullivan's."

Wide-eyed, Lili shook her head. "I do not want to do anything to make Mr. Eldridge more angry. I need his help to postpone the management meeting."

"Actually, you don't have to break Sullivan's Rules," Rita said. "All you have to do is bend them a little to make them work for you. Heck, if I hadn't bent a couple, I wouldn't be with Colby now."

"There are so many rules to remember," Lili said as Arthur, the office gofer, came around the corner pushing his refreshment cart. The last thing she wanted was for her situation to become office gossip. "Which of Sullivan's Rules are you talking about?" she whispered.

"Rule number five, or for that matter, all of them," Rita replied, carefully eyeing Arthur's progress down the hall. "They all seem to advise a woman to try to make a man feel masculine."

Lili's eyes widened. "How?"

"By showing him how much you like and appreciate him," April said.

Rita leaned closer to Lili. "Of course, it's only part of rule five you need to think about. I'm sure you realize from your own experience that if you sublimate your own desires and allow things to happen naturally, you're never going to get anywhere with a man like Tom."

As Lili nodded solemnly, the subject of their conversation approached them. The three women froze.

"Good morning, ladies," Tom said amiably as he eyed Lili. "I hope this is a business meeting."

With that not-so-subtle warning, and without waiting for an answer, he raised an eyebrow and walked away.

TOM FELT THREE PAIRS of disapproving eyes boring into his back as he walked down the hall. If not for Lili's crusade, he wouldn't have thought about the survival of the day care center. He actually felt sorry about the situation, but it was out of his hands.

Besides, beyond polite conversation, or, he admitted reluctantly, sometimes not so polite conversation, fraternizing with his staff outside office hours had been a no-no ever since he'd taken over as publisher. His father may have considered all his employees as one big happy family, but not him. It only led to trouble. Lili was a case in point.

Besides, managing the magazine took most of his waking hours. The last thing he needed was to have Riverview's management raise the figures on his lease agreement or, perish the thought, cancel the lease when it came up for renewal next month.

If only the magazine's annual employee picnic wasn't coming up next Sunday, he would have felt easier about the future. If he'd read Lili's determined body language correctly, he was going to have to listen to a hell of a lot of arguments from her about keeping the day care open, and the picnic would provide her with the perfect opportunity to corner him.

TOM PASTED A SMILE on his face as he politely greeted employees arriving for *Today's World*'s annual picnic.

In no time, the magazine's staff, their families and friends were scattered over the lush green meadow in Lincoln Park, enjoying games and each other's company. Overhead, the sky was cloudless, and the temperature had climbed into the seventies.

Just his luck, Tom thought as he shook another hand and acknowledged another greeting. He might have wished for a late spring rain to break up the picnic early, but the sun was shining brightly, the flowers were blooming and the trees were sprouting buds.

Since Lili and her friends were undoubtedly out there formenting trouble, he intended to keep a close eye on the day's activities. At the moment, things were going so well, he found himself waiting uneasily for the first sign of a problem.

Sure enough, it came with a bang, but not in the way he'd expected.

"Look out!"

At the frantic shout, Tom ducked instinctively. Considering there were at least three different ball games going on in front of him, he wasn't sure what he was supposed to watch out for. A baseball? A soccer ball? A volley ball?

He found out the hard way when he was hit squarely in the groin by a black-and-white soccer ball apparently hurled into space by an energetic player.

With a muffled curse, he caught the ball before it had a chance to roll away. To his mortification, the private part of him he preferred to keep private hurt like hell.

Tom glanced down at the wet ball he held and noticed the large glob of brown mud smeared across the fly of his shorts. If he'd hoped to keep the point of contact a secret, he was out of luck.

A little girl, cheeks flushed with sun and excitement, her blond ponytail flying out behind her, skidded to a stop in front of him.

"Sorry mister. The ball was going too fast. I couldn't kick it the other way!"

Tom took a series of deep breaths until the red haze in front of his eyes cleared. The blow might have been an accident, but the region south of his belt hurt like hell. The rest of him, including his head, was pounding in sympathy. Still, he tried to keep his cool.

He surveyed the apologetic half-pint in front of him. There was no use being angry. He could recognize innocence when he saw it.

Besides, with so many games going on, he should have been more alert. If he'd been hit in the head with the same force, he would have been knocked out like a light.

Fortunately, the pain in his groin was dulling to a steady throb. He moved gingerly to test the results of his injury and sighed with relief. He might not be home free, but everything seemed to be in working order.

Before he had a chance to tell the kid not to worry, that he was sure he'd live, a young woman came charging across the field toward him.

Lili Soulé.

How much worse could the day get? Tom wondered bleakly.

Chapter Two

"I am so sorry, Mr. Eldridge—er, Tom," Lili said distractedly, remembering Rita's instructions to call him by his first name. "I am sure my daughter didn't mean for the ball to hit you. Paulette, apologize to Mr. Eldridge this minute!"

Tom took another deep breath to control what was left of the pain. "No problem, she's already apologized."

For a moment, the thought crossed his mind that Lili might have deliberately set him up to teach him a lesson in humility. He eyed her cautiously. "I'm sure it was an accident. I suppose I could say it was my fault—I should have kept well away from the playing field."

"Oh no," Lili said worriedly. "Paulette has to learn to be more careful when she's playing ball. Unfortunately, this has happened before," she added with a stern look at her daughter.

"I'll live." Tom cautiously shifted from one foot to another, trying to find the most comfortable position. To his chagrin, the muddy spot on his shorts shifted with him.

How in the hell would he be able to look her in the eyes at the office tomorrow?

"If I continue to hang around here, I have a feeling this isn't going to be the only time I'll get in the way of a bouncing ball," Tom added, hoping to displace Lili's horrified gaze. The pain was bad enough that he could have cursed a blue streak, but he realized a child was present. "Nice day for a picnic, isn't it?" he said inanely. Lili blinked and the kid grinned, but her humor was short-lived as her mother turned to lecture her about paying attention to what she was doing.

Tom listened to Lili read her daughter the riot act, wondering as he did how he could ever have thought of this lovely woman as serene.

He watched the way the afternoon breeze was sending wisps of her silky blond hair across her sapphire eyes. And wondered at her tender smile, even as she continued to warn her daughter about the safety aspects of playing soccer.

The more he studied Lili, the more fascinating he found her to be. How could he ever have thought her fragile and uninteresting?

He glanced at her left hand—no wedding ring. Just as he'd thought. It would be dangerous for a man like him to become involved with a single mother with small children.

Uneasy at the direction of his thoughts, he began to wonder if fate in the shape of a bouncing soccer ball had deliberately set him up.

"Sorry, mister," the kid finally said. "I gotta go now. My friends want the ball!" She grabbed the soccer ball out of his hands and, before her mother could stop her, took off at a run.

Lili blew her daughter a kiss, then turned back to Tom. "I'm afraid there is no way for me to contain my

daughter's enthusiasm for sports. She has been a tom-
boy from the time she learned to walk."

"Like I said before, I'm okay," Tom answered her,
even though shafts of pain coursed through him every
time he took a deep breath. If he hadn't already known
from the days he'd played football that getting hit in the
groin was as bad as it could get, he sure knew it now.

Lili frowned as she glanced at the beads of moisture
that had gathered on Tom's forehead. "I *knew* you were
hurt. I have an idea. Wait here and don't move," she ordered when he tried to interrupt. "I'll be back in a minute with something to help you."

Her eye-catching yellow sundress flashed brightly as
she made for an ice cream truck parked on the asphalt
a few yards away.

Ice cream? Tom frowned. What made her think an
ice cream treat would do anything for the pain running
through him?

As if nearly being gelded in the prime of life wasn't
enough, he still had the problem of what to do about this
woman and her crusade.

Tom turned as he heard a familiar voice shout at him
from across the playing field, and saw his father head-
ing in his direction. Apparently fate was further intent
on complicating his life. Judging by his dad's determined body language as he made his way through the
crowd, Tom was afraid he was going to have to listen
to another of his lectures.

Seeing Tom in the company of a woman like Lili and
her small daughter was bound to have drawn his dad's
attention. Tom prepared himself for a speech on the
joys of marriage and fatherhood. Not that it would be
the first time his father had sounded off about Tom's sin-

gle state. Homer Eldridge made no secret that he wanted grandchildren before it was too late for him to enjoy them. Even if they came ready-made.

Tom's younger sister, Megan, bless her cowardly heart, was still single, too, but as a travel writer, she made a point of touching home base as seldom as possible. At the moment, she was busy flying around the world researching articles for a local newspaper. A side benefit was that her work kept her as far away from their father's matchmaking activities as possible. The last time Tom had heard from Megan, she'd been somewhere in Bali, sunning herself and admiring the local males from a safe distance. To further rile him, she'd congratulated herself on having no dependents the last time she'd called.

He should have insisted Megan return home and at least help run the letters-to-the-editor pages of the magazine. So much mail had come in since they'd published Lucas Sullivan's controversial article. And maybe if Megan were around, their father's attention would turn from Tom to his sister.

Still, Tom counted himself lucky. If Megan, a well-intentioned do-gooder, had been living in Chicago, even without children of her own, she would have been all over him, insisting he help Lili keep the day care open. It was bad enough the management was up in arms because of Lili's escapades; the last thing Tom needed was having Megan on his back.

Maybe he hadn't made himself clear the last time he'd told his father he wasn't cut out for the marriage game, and even less for fatherhood. If he hadn't already been convinced that he was a contented bachelor, Tom had become a true believer when he'd commissioned

Lucas, his fraternity brother, to write "Sullivan's Rules." The article had convinced Tom he was right: a strong woman was to be avoided at all costs.

He thought of Sullivan's Rule number five, which called for a woman to "show her man how much she likes and appreciates him." It was right on the mark.

He gazed after Lili. Number six, on second thought, wasn't bad, either. He would have been happy with a woman who was "supportive, fun-loving, easygoing, and generous in her praise of a man's achievements." Just not today.

He wasn't the only one uninterested in fatherhood, he told himself righteously. Not one of Sullivan's Rules mentioned children.

Tom cautiously eyed the way Lili and the ice cream vendor were deep in conversation. Injured or not, his body still stirred at the sight of Lili's shapely bare legs. The hem of her short dress rose even higher as she gestured to the vendor, leaning over the counter in the side of his truck.

It would have taken a man of iron not to admire Lili's exquisite knees and the glimpse of golden thighs.

Thank God, Tom thought as he felt his body stir. His vital parts were still working.

On the other hand, something had to be wrong for him to be reacting this way. Now that he knew Lili was leading the crusade to keep the center open, how could he possibly be lusting after her? And then there was his policy of no fraternizing with members of his staff.

If he was suffering a severe case of spring fever, he'd have to do something to take his mind off Lili.

He also had to do something fast to get rid of her before his dad made it all the way across the playing field.

But parts of Tom still hurt too much to hurry, and a quick mental calculation told him he would never make it to the ice cream truck and back before his father arrived. Besides, how could he reject the woman's efforts to help him?

Another problem was the way she'd taken to calling him Tom instead of her usual "Mr. Eldridge" in that intriguing accent. Intriguing enough to send his thoughts down paths he'd deliberately managed to avoid until now.

He turned back to check on his father's progress, but Homer had stopped to admire a baby. Tom noticed Paulette streaking after another soccer ball and desperately looked around for some shrub where he could hide.

Before he could take refuge, Lili came hurrying up to him. "Now," she said briskly as she glanced around the grassy area, "all we need to do is find a place for you to lie down."

Lying down sounded like a good idea, Tom thought wryly as he put his weight on both legs. The problem was that he would be in plain sight for his father to spot him. The bigger problem was the brown paper bag Lili carried.

"Why?" he asked warily, even though he admitted that under difference circumstances, lying down with Lili might have been an idea worth considering.

"So that I can help you!"

To his dismay, she was gazing quizzically at his shorts.

"Help me?" Tom eyed the leaking brown bag. "If that's what I think it is, I have to tell you I'm not in the mood for ice cream just now. Thanks, anyway."

"No." Lili smiled at what she obviously thought was his attempt at a joke.

If she only knew he wasn't trying to be funny.

"When I told the ice cream vendor what had happened, he was kind enough to give me some ice cubes to ease your pain. I didn't have any way to carry them, so he gave me this bag. Now, come with me," she added. "As soon as we can find a place away from the ball field, I will apply the ice to your injury."

Tom shivered at the thought of having Lili anywhere near his aching groin.

He tried putting his weight on his right foot. A sharp pain shot down his legs. "I'm sure I'll be fine without the ice. Just give me another minute."

"You are sure?" Lili eyed him dubiously. "Ice always helps Paulette when she scrapes her knee."

"If it were my knee, Lili, I'd let you apply the ice cubes," Tom said fervently. "As it is…" He hesitated at her blush. There was no way he could come up with a creative way to describe his injury without embarrassing them both.

It was time to compromise.

He glanced around the surrounding area. Letting Lili help him hide from his father sounded like a good idea, but that was as far as he was willing to go. Unfortunately, the only place to lie down, short of staggering back to his car, appeared to be on the other side of a grassy knoll a few yards away. He took a deep breath.

"Toss the ice cubes and follow me."

To his dismay, after Lili tossed the bag of ice cubes behind a tree, she hurried to put her arm around his waist as he slowly made his way up and over the small embankment. He tried leaning away from her, but it wasn't working. Even the lingering pain that ran through him couldn't distract him from her sweet scent, earnest blue eyes and the determined set of her lips.

Tom swallowed a groan. The last thing he needed was Lili's close proximity to remind him that while he might be mentally ready and willing, he wasn't able.

"There." Lili stopped and admired a lush patch of grass. "Now, stretch out, please."

Tom still wasn't convinced it was the brightest idea he'd ever had, but he let her help him sink to the ground. Once on his back, he closed his eyes and tried to relax, but nothing short of a tornado could have kept him from being aware of Lili.

"Just let me rest for a few minutes." He threw an arm over his eyes to block out the strong sun shining down on him, and the look of concern in Lili's eyes. The last time he'd experienced such tender loving care had been as a kid at his late mother's knee, he thought fleetingly. But he was sure as hell a long way from thinking of Lili as his mother.

"You are certain you are going to be okay without the ice cubes?" Lili asked when she saw him wince. "I can always go back and get more."

Between Lili's attempt to help him and his father's determination to see him married, Tom was beginning to feel like a goose being fattened up for dinner.

A child's voice broke into his reverie. "Mama? Is the man going to be okay?"

Tom opened his eyes to see two wide hazel eyes gazing down at him with sympathy. Recognizing the kid's shorts and shirt, he mustered a smile. "Don't worry. I'm okay, Paulette."

The kid frowned. "I'm not Paulette."

Beside him, Lili giggled, a happy, tinkling laugh

that, if he hadn't felt like a fool, would have brought a smile to Tom's face. "This isn't Paulette."

"No?" He shaded his eyes against the blinding sunlight. A closer look revealed a small boy with short blond hair instead of a golden ponytail.

"Don't tell me there are two of you!" Tom groaned, then remembered Lili had mentioned twins. The thought that not one but two small children came with Lili was overwhelming. For a man who'd had almost nothing to do with kids for most of his adult life, he wasn't sure how to apologize to the boy.

"Yes," Lili replied, smiling fondly at the newcomer. "This is Paul, Paulette's twin brother."

"You don't happen to have a soccer ball on you, do you?" Tom asked eying the boy warily.

Paul shook his head. "My sister plays soccer. I like action figures. I'm going to be an artist like my mother when I grow up."

Tom smothered a sigh of relief, closed his eyes again and tried to pretend he was somewhere else. Somewhere nice and quiet where there were no soccer balls to dodge and no need for ice cubes to cool his overheated, aching body. And no children.

He must have fallen asleep for a few minutes, because the last thing he remembered was Lili leaning over him. The spaghetti straps holding up her body-hugging sundress drooped over creamy shoulders. In the hollow between her breasts, a single gold chain nestled, and wisps of blond hair fell over her forehead and tickled his nose.

The next time he opened his eyes, Lili was sitting cross-legged at his side and eating an ice cream cone. A few feet away, Paul was on his hands and knees investigating a gopher hole. To Tom's amusement, the gopher turned out to be as curious about Paul as Paul was about him, and they almost bumped noses. Tom wasn't sure who was the more surprised, the gopher or Paul.

Tom found himself laughing. By his side, Lili laughed, too. Judging from her loving glance, it was obvious she felt that children were a joy and a blessing, not a nuisance.

Tom realized that to strangers passing by, they must look like a normal family enjoying a picnic in the park.

Lili's twins were cute, and he had a feeling that all it would take was a few more moments like this to make him forget Sullivan's Rules calling for caution in male-female relationships.

Maybe the attraction was simply because he was vulnerable.

"Ah, so there you are!" Homer Eldridge beamed as he made his way over the grassy rise. "I lost sight of you for a while, but I knew that if I looked hard enough I'd find you."

Tom smothered a groan.

Trouble had a way of following him, he mused as he tried to sit up. The picture of Lili, little Paul and him sitting together had apparently been enough to bring a smile to his father's face. Tom hadn't seen Homer so happy in years.

Happy was good, Tom thought with compassion as he gazed at his dad. Homer had been in the dumps ever since he'd talked himself into retiring from *Today's World*, ostensibly to give Tom the opportunity to make his mark on the magazine. More likely, Tom suspected, his father had wanted to encourage him to settle down— in both his professional and personal life.

"Married with children" had become a broken record.

"Sorry I didn't get up, Dad." Tom explained to his father about the errant soccer ball. "I feel a little better now.

"By the way," he added, remembering he wasn't alone. "I guess I should introduce you to Lili Soulé. Lili is the magazine's graphic artist. Lili, this is my dad, Homer Eldridge."

"I remember seeing you around the magazine once or twice before I retired, Ms. Soulé," his father said, smiling as he reached to take Lili's offered hand. "Glad to meet you. You don't mind my calling you Lili, do you? Especially seeing that you and Tom are friends?"

Lili blushed. "I am pleased to meet you, too, Mr. Eldridge. You may call me Lili if you wish."

Tom's father gestured to Paul. "Your son?"

"Yes," Lili said proudly. "Paul is a twin. His sister is out there somewhere playing soccer. I'm afraid it was Paulette who kicked the ball that hit Tom."

Homer glanced over his shoulder at the soccer field, which was rimmed by shouting children and cheering parents. "And the children's father? Is he here today?"

Lili's smile faded. "I lost my husband, Paul, four years ago in an accident," she said softly. "Little Paul here is now the man of the family."

Tom's father murmured in sympathy. "And a fine young man he is. How old is he?"

"He is six," Lili replied. Obviously wondering at the senior Eldridge's sudden interest in her son, she glanced at Tom with a raised eyebrow. Hoping he was wrong about his father's interest, Tom managed a shrug.

"Ah, yes," Homer replied with a fond smile. "Still,

every boy needs a father to help him along the road to manhood. Don't you agree?"

Even as Tom shook his head, Lili nodded.

Judging from his father's benevolent smile, Tom had a sinking feeling his dad had decided Lili and her twins would not only make a perfect family, but provide him with instant grandchildren.

In a way, Homer was right, Tom mused as a becoming flush pinkened Lili's cheeks. Tom was a red-blooded man and Lili was definitely all woman. If only she hadn't displayed such a will of steel and relentless determination. He knew from experience that a strong woman spelled trouble.

He was also old-fashioned enough to believe that his frat brother, Lucas Sullivan, had been right in his article on the mating game. A woman had to let a man set the pace in their relationship, or at least allow him to be a partner. Since he'd discovered the real Lili, Tom wasn't sure she was ready to do either.

He intended to get around to marriage someday, maybe, but not yet. If his father was so set on being a grandfather, maybe there was still a chance that his sister would develop a nesting instinct, marry and provide the grandchildren.

Impatiently, he listened while his father and Lili exchanged pleasantries. The longer the two spoke, the broader the smile on his father's face became. Not a good sign.

"Tom," Homer finally suggested, "why don't you bring Lili and the children over to my place for dinner next Friday?"

Tom was about to say he had another engagement when the activity on the ball fields stopped and picnic-goers broke into whistles and shouts. Slowly, he swiveled to see what had prompted the outburst. It seemed as if everyone was looking skyward, pointing and cheering. To Tom's dismay, a small plane flew overhead, trailing a large yellow banner: HELP KEEP RIVERVIEW CHILD CARE CENTER OPEN!

A deep foreboding washed over Tom. He knew, as sure as he knew his own name, that his life was about to become even more complicated.

Chapter Three

This had to be Lili's doing.

Today's stunt with the plane had to be just another way to rev up her crusade to save the center. But this time she'd gone too far. It was beginning to look as if her wide-ranging imagination greatly exceeded her charm.

Gritting his teeth to hide his frustration, Tom turned to a wide-eyed Lili and gestured to the banner. "You?"

"Mais non!" To Lili's chagrin, whenever she became agitated, she reverted to her native language. How could Tom think she'd hired the airplane? He had to know she couldn't have afforded to do that even if she'd wanted to.

"You're sure about that?"

Lili nodded. To her dismay, what had begun as a campaign intended solely for the Riverview Building's tenants must surely be known to most of Chicago by now. The realization that the local papers and television stations were bound to pick up on the flyover made her knees grow weak. Judging from the look on Tom's face, it would be a miracle if she wasn't fired.

"Any idea who *is* behind it?" Tom demanded between clenched teeth. "If I do find out who did it…" He left the sentence unfinished, but his threat was clear.

Lili's blood ran cold as the airplane flew out of sight. She was innocent, but she had the feeling that the brains behind this caper belonged to one or both of her friends, Rita and April. And it was only a matter of time before Tom found the culprit.

Her lips were sealed.

She sensed Tom's frustration in the rigid way he held himself. Whatever he was thinking couldn't be good.

It wasn't only her own job on the line, she realized as she gazed up, to discover the plane had reappeared. Her campaign might come back to bite her friends, as well.

"What's all the shouting about?" Tom's father asked.

Wordlessly, Tom pointed skyward.

Homer Eldridge shaded his eyes and gazed upward to the accompaniment of hoots, whistles and shouts from everyone on the playing field.

"Who's trying to close our day care center?" Homer demanded. "Better yet, who's behind that stunt? I'd like to have a few words with them!"

Lili was afraid from the thunderous look on his face that the senior Eldridge intended to give any perpetrators hell. Well, for that matter, so did Tom if he found them. And from the way he was glaring at the airplane, it was going to be soon.

"In answer to your first question, Dad," Tom began with a scowl at Lili, "I'm damn sure that the reason for the plane is that Jules Kagan has called a meeting to discuss closing the center. If you ask me, it's already a done deal—" he shot a telling look at Lili "—even if some people don't want to believe it.

"As for the person behind that misguided stunt up there," Tom added, "I'm not sure who it is, but I have a good idea."

Homer Eldridge's face grew mottled with anger as he stared at the banner flying overhead. "You have it all wrong, Son. I'm not angry at whoever hired the plane. Considering I was one of the tenants that started the day care, I should have been told Jules wants to close the place down. If I'd known, I would have tried to stop that fool exhibition up there before it got started. No matter how well intentioned the perpetrator might be, I'm afraid there's going to be hell to pay when Kagan finds out!"

"Don't worry, Dad." Tom sent another pointed look at Lili. "I'm pretty sure I know who's behind the stunt. I plan on taking care of it the first thing in the morning."

"Hell, you're not listening!" his father retorted. "That's not what I meant. If it weren't for Jules's reaction, I'd be tempted to give whoever's behind the stunt a medal. As it is, this will only make matters worse."

Gazing at Tom, Lili saw the warm, velvety brown eyes that she considered so sensuous grow cool. Another bad sign.

"You know as well as I do, Dad, that our lease renewal is coming up soon," Tom continued. "If we do anything else to antagonize Kagan, it's only going to cost us."

His father snorted and loosened the collar of his shirt from around his burly neck. "It's getting too damn hot out here and I have a strong feeling it's going to get a lot hotter before this mess is over. Things have already gone too far."

He glanced over at Paul, who was busy poking a twig down the gopher hole. "I take it your boy attends the day care center, Lili?"

Lili ignored Tom's warning look. She could use all the help she could get. "Yes, he does," she said proudly. "Paul and his sister were in Riverview's day care until they started public school. They are in afternoon care there now."

Homer's frown grew deeper for a moment, then he smiled. "The fact you have children there makes the problem more personal. Don't you worry, my dear, you can leave everything to me. I'll take care of this."

"Come on, Dad." Tom broke in, concerned about the subtext in his father's satisfied smile. The man was obviously taken by Lili, but the less he became involved with her and her children, the better. "You're retired now, Dad. You ought to be enjoying yourself instead of working yourself into a heart attack over this. Like I said, just leave the details to me."

"Some details," Homer muttered as the plane circled the park one last time, dipped its wings in a salute to the watchers below, and in a sputter of staccato sound disappeared from view. "I said I'll take care of this and I will. Where's your cell phone?"

Tom sighed, dug in his pocket and handed over his phone. "It's Sunday. I don't think you'll be able to reach anyone today."

"We'll see about that!" his father retorted. "Hell, Jules Kagan had better talk to me! We go back too far for him to ignore me now. If I have to, I'll remind him that I was one of the first businesses to sign a lease when he became owner of the Riverview. I even brought a couple of other prospective tenants with me to raise the occupancy rate so he could impress the bankers when he applied for a loan."

Homer stopped to gaze reassuringly at Lili. "Now, excuse me while I take this conversation somewhere private. I wouldn't want to offend your ears." He stomped across the grass and over the slight rise, then disappeared from sight.

Since she was one of the prime movers in the campaign to save the center, Lili felt guiltier than ever. She'd asked her friends for help, but she'd never expected them to hire an airplane to advertise her crusade. Knowing the way Rita's mind worked, maybe Lili should have taken the time to make them promise to keep her in the loop before they went this far.

The way Tom looked, she knew he didn't believe she'd had nothing to do with hiring the airplane. But she had to try again.

"I am so sorry, Tom. No matter how I feel, I never intended for something like this to happen. Or," she added as the annoyed look Homer had shot Tom flashed through her mind, "to cause a problem between you and your father."

"Yeah, sure," Tom replied, trying to focus on his anger instead of the way Lili's sundress hugged her lush curves.

He might be frustrated with the woman, but he was also fully aware of her charms. There was something special about Lili he couldn't ignore.

"If you weren't the one who cooked up that stunt," he said, forcing himself back to the issue at hand, "how about telling me whose bird-brained idea it was?"

Homer Eldridge stormed back into view before Lili could answer. "That damn fool won't give me the time of day! Says he saw the plane fly over his penthouse on the other side of the park! He sounded mad as hell!"

"Will he close the center over this?" Dismayed, Lili couldn't hide her anguish. Now that the Riverview's owner was directly involved, things had gone too far. From what Tom's father was saying, the chances of reversing the man's mind didn't appear any more likely than finding some way to placate Tom himself.

"The damn fool threatened to close it, but don't worry, Lili," Eldridge said soothingly. "I'll get to Jules sooner or later and make him see the light or my name isn't Homer Eldridge! As a matter of fact," he added with a glare at the high-rise building that towered above the trees, "I'm going over and make him talk to me right now or I'll break down his door trying. As for you, Son," Eldridge said before he stomped away, "don't forget you're going to bring Lili and her children to dinner on Friday. I'm expecting you."

Troubled at the reason for the invitation, Tom waited until his father was out of sight to tackle Lili. "We have to talk."

She swallowed the lump in her throat. The moment she'd feared had obviously arrived. She'd wanted Tom to notice her the way a man notices a woman, not the way he was looking at her now. "Talk about what?"

"Us," Tom answered succinctly. "And now, before the situation goes too far."

"There is an us?" Confused by the intimacy the word implied, she locked her gaze with Tom's. How could there be an "us" when it was clear he was angry with her?

"Yeah, us," Tom said. "But before we get started, I have a question. You don't really want to go to my father's for dinner Friday, do you?"

"I *am* a little surprised at his invitation," Lili confessed warily. She didn't want to be responsible for creating any more friction between Tom and his father. The threat of the day care closing had fired up both Eldridges enough.

Still, no matter what other reasons Homer had for inviting her and the children, Lili had too much at stake surrounding the center to ignore his offer of help.

If the center closed, she might have to consider returning to her family in France. But in her heart she knew she could never do that. She'd promised her late husband to raise their children as Americans when he was critically injured in an automobile accident.

"I will not accept your father's invitation if it will cause trouble between the two of you," she finally answered. "But first we need to talk about my trying to keep the day care open. I must be honest with you. I appreciate your concern, but I cannot stop my campaign."

"Maybe so, but we still have to talk."

"About the center?"

Tom nodded. "Yeah, but that can wait for later. Right now, I think we have a bigger problem to take care of."

Puzzled, Lili clasped her hands to keep them from trembling. What was more important than saving the day care?

Sensing Tom's obvious reluctance to go on, she finally spoke up. "If this is not about the center, then it has to be about me. If you wish to fire me now, you may go ahead. But I hope you will reconsider."

Tom's expression grew grim. "Like I said, that's not what I want to talk about. What I have to say concerns a personal matter."

"Say what you feel you must," she said bravely,

knowing that whether the problem was personal or professional, it would still affect her job.

Tom took a deep breath and looked around to make sure his father was safely out of sight. "Well, if you're sure… I suppose I might as well be frank with you. The problem between my dad and me concerns wedding bells. And now that he's seen you, I'm afraid you're part of it."

"I do not understand this wedding bells," Lili said with a puzzled frown, her head cocked to one side. "I think it refers to marriage, but what does it have to do with me? I am not about to get married."

Tom raked his fingers through his hair in frustration. He was too old to be asking a woman for a date, even if he didn't intend it to be a real one. Hell, as his father kept reminding him, most men his age were already married with children. "You're right. The problem is more about me than it is about you."

Relieved, but still puzzled, Lili nodded cautiously.

"You might not believe this," Tom began, "but the invitation is actually about my father wanting me to marry and start a family. Grandchildren are all he talks about whenever we're together. Now that he's seen us and your son together, I'm afraid he's gotten the wrong idea. I have a gut feeling he sees a chance for the family he wants me to have."

Relieved at the mention of grandchildren, Lili nodded in understanding. "Of course. Every parent wishes this for their children—a happy family. I cannot imagine life without my little ones. My younger brother, who lives in France, married young and is the father of five children. If my own Paul had survived," she added with a shy smile, "perhaps I would have matched Christopher's record by now."

She couldn't bring herself to ask Tom how old he was or why he hadn't married. In spite of what Rita had said about him being interested only in the magazine, Lili remembered the light in his eyes when he'd looked at her. And besides, Tom was a very sexy man. It was a wonder some woman hadn't managed to lead him to the altar by now.

"I am sorry, but I still do not see where I enter into this problem of wedding bells," she said. "You are my employer, but we know very little about each other. We are still almost strangers."

"Right," Tom agreed with a cautious glance at the playing field, where the children had gone back to their soccer game. "It's just that I noticed my father's reaction after he met you and saw Paul." He took a deep breath. "I know this may sound strange to you, but I'm afraid Dad sees you as a likely marriage prospect for me."

Lili blinked. Being the target of the senior Eldridge's matchmaking plans for Tom was surprising, and yet it touched her, too. Homer Eldridge must be a very caring father to be so concerned about his son's happiness.

The realization that Tom was actually *afraid* she was being considered as a suitable marriage partner for him brought a pang of regret to her heart.

If only she hadn't been so foolish as to have the same impossible dream, she would have been able to laugh off the senior Eldridge's interest in her as merely an amusing idea. What wasn't amusing was Tom's reaction to his father's dinner invitation. She might wish to be in Tom's arms, making love with him, but it was crystal clear that he did not share such a dream.

She tried to smile away the growing tension she felt

between them. "I am sure your father is only trying to be kind. If you wish, I will call and give him my regrets."

Tom shook his head. "If you knew my father as well as I do, you'd know it's not that easy. I know I have a reputation around the magazine for being stubborn," he added with a wry smile, "but my father has me beat. Dad's a pro at getting his way."

"But he's never met me before today," Lili protested. "I am not the easygoing woman I appear to be. If I were, I would never have managed to take care of myself and the children these past four years."

Tom studied Lili. He, too, had underestimated her. Strong when he'd thought her mild mannered, wise when he'd thought her merely opinionated, Lili was not only beautiful and intelligent but self-reliant and capable. And, judging from the fire in her exquisite eyes, sensually exciting.

He couldn't understand his muddled thinking. A month ago, he'd hardly noticed her. Well, maybe a little on his occasional visits to the art department. But he sure noticed her now.

A week ago, he'd actually warned her to stop causing trouble. Now, in spite of the ache in his groin that should have turned him off even thinking sexually about Lili, he was still physically attracted to her. Go figure.

He *was* sure of one thing. He had to put this attraction to her out of his mind. She was his employee. He had to remember he had a magazine to publish, a magazine his father had, with his easygoing management style, left hanging over a cliff marked Bankruptcy. Even though publishing "Sullivan's Rules" had turned the magazine around, this was no time to be thinking of a real relationship.

Now that he had Sullivan's Rules to guide him, if and when he became ready for a lasting relationship, Tom would know better than to fall for a five-foot-three, fiercely independent female.

The problem was he couldn't ignore Lili's sparkling eyes, her silky golden hair or those lips surely meant for kissing.

"I'm afraid it's not going to be easy to turn down Dad's invitation," Tom finally said in answer to her questioning gaze. "Especially since it appears he shares your concern for the center. Now that Dad's involved himself in the problem, he'll think it strange if you don't accept his invitation to dinner."

"Is that all you wished to tell me?" Lili asked, on edge and anxious to leave before Tom remembered why he'd been angry with her. "I must go. The children are hungry. I have to give them their lunch."

"Wait a minute, please," he said, anxious to discuss the sensitive issue while he still had the nerve. He touched Lili's elbow. A big mistake. Touching her warm skin only made him more aware of her than ever.

"Has it occurred to you that maybe my father's scheme to involve me with you and your kids could turn out to benefit both of us?"

Wide-eyed, Lili stared at him. "Your father's interest in me as your future wife is a good thing?"

"Yes." Tom flushed at the skepticism in her voice, but hurried on. "I know it sounds crazy, but try to see things my way. If I bring you to dinner Friday and give the impression we're an item, he'll lay off needling me to get married. He's bound to let nature take its course. And he'll do everything he can to support your case to keep the center open."

Aware that Tom's interest in her wasn't the kind she'd wished for, Lili still found herself considering his strange proposal.

How could she turn her back on a man who had every right to fire her for causing him problems, but had not?

How could she turn her back on the man her heart and soul had yearned for these past two years, even though she now knew her feelings were not reciprocated?

"I will have to think about this," she finally replied, her mind whirling at Tom's proposal. "But not about this talk of engagements and wedding bells," she added firmly. "If I decide to go to dinner with you, it will only be as your date for the evening, nothing more."

Tom was disappointed. Being seen with Lili for only one night wasn't going to cut it. His father would need more than that to stop pressuring Tom. "You're sure about that?"

"Yes. I must make certain your father realizes I have too many responsibilities to even consider such a commitment. I will bring the twins to prove the point. Agreed?"

What she didn't add was that even if he did reciprocate her feelings, she would never consider marrying a man who seemed so uncomfortable with children.

"You'd bring the twins?"

Lili nodded. "Your father did invite them."

Tom swallowed a groan. Children creating bedlam in a park were harmless—if you didn't count his encounter with the soccer ball, that is. The thought of little Paul investigating Homer's precious collection of Mayan artifacts was actually frightening. As for the athletic Paulette, heaven only knew what havoc she might create in his father's penthouse before the evening was through.

"Are you really sure you'd want to bring the twins?" he asked, glancing at the lively soccer game still going on. "Kids don't seem to sit still for very long."

Once again Lili realized how very limited Tom's experience with children was. No wonder he couldn't relate to her fight to try to keep the center open.

"That's true," she agreed with a smile. "I'm sure your father will change his mind about wanting ready-made grandchildren when he sees how active my twins are."

Even active children wouldn't change his father's mind, Tom thought, but he said nothing. Homer had been too busy to share Tom's interest in baseball when Tom was growing up, but it looked as if his father was determined to have grandchildren while he was still spry enough to enjoy them. Even lively stepgrandchildren would make him deliriously happy.

Tom had no choice. He had to tell Lili he was willing to go along with her plan to bring her children to dinner Friday night, and let the future take care of itself. And while the twins made his father happy, he would have a chance to get to know Lili outside working hours.

That included finding out how to keep her out of trouble while trying to think of a way to help in her crusade.

No sooner had Lili started to answer than Paul gave up his pursuit of the gopher and ran back to his mother. "Mama, I'm hungry."

"Yes, of course." She ruffled her son's hair with a fond smile. "Find your sister and tell her we are about to have lunch. I will meet you by our blanket in a few minutes." She held out her hand to Tom. "I am truly sorry for your accident," she said somberly. "I hope you will feel better before Friday."

"Actually, I feel great now that I've laid out the problem with my father." Tom took Lili's extended hand— another big mistake. Her warm, satiny skin sent his thoughts down roads he hadn't intended to travel anytime soon, and especially not with a woman who seemed determined to go her own way. "I'll see you back at the office in the morning. Then," he added in a much more somber tone, "we'll talk about finding who hired the airplane."

Lili hid her uneasiness with a smile. She was sure Tom would track down the person who'd hired the airplane, and read her the riot act, but not if Lili found her first.

"About dinner," Tom continued. "Are you sure you want to do this?"

Pretending to be Tom's date might fulfill a fantasy of hers, Lili thought, but how could she hide her true feelings for him in the process?

"If the idea of pretending to be my date bothers you, then forget it, Lili," Tom said when she remained silent. "I just thought I could make my father happy, and we'd both get what we wanted out of this."

"What we both wanted?" For a moment Lili forgot about the day care and feared Tom must know how she felt about him. She began to regret her impulsive response to the dinner invitation.

"Sure," Tom said. "I'd have a pretend fiancée, and

you'd have my protection if Riverview's management found out you were the brains behind the protest." He studied her closely. "That is, if you stayed out of trouble."

Lili swallowed the lump in her throat at the veiled threat. As far as she could tell, she needed protection from Tom rather than from the building's management. Well, she thought with a determined smile, two could play this game.

She met his questioning gaze with a direct look of her own and wondered how she could set matters straight with him and still go on with her crusade. Maybe he thought she was naive about male-female relationships. What he didn't realize was that French-women knew all there was to know about the mating game. They'd invented it.

"I will think more about this bargain you speak of," she told Tom, trying to ignore the hollow feeling in her middle. "I will give you my answer tomorrow at work."

"Is that a yes?"

"No." Lili returned her son's wave. "It is a maybe."

Chapter Four

The Riverview's cafeteria was humming at noon on Monday. Not with the usual office gossip, but with a spirited debate on who could have initiated yesterday's sensational plane flyover at Lincoln Park. Some people thought it was intended to be a joke, others a conspiracy. But apparently everyone agreed the stunt had been the highlight of the employees' annual picnic.

Lili was pleased to hear that the debate wasn't limited to *Today's World* staff. There was some conjecture about possible consequences if the culprit was found, but the general feeling seemed to be that more people would be joining in the effort to keep the center open. There was even talk that if the management didn't see the light, some kind of strike should be organized!

She made her way to a table in the far corner where she, April and Rita usually met for lunch. Lili was pretty sure Rita was the person who had hired the plane, and she was planning to confront her in their secluded niche.

As she took her seat, Lili studied the initials on a heart someone had carved into the wooden tabletop— the same table where she and her friends had at one time plotted April's successful conquest of Lucas Sullivan.

Ditto for Rita's unexpected marriage to former Texas Ranger Colby Callahan, which had been followed by a honeymoon in Bermuda.

If only the corner didn't carry so many romantic memories, Lili thought wistfully. For her, it was a constant reminder of her unrealistic attraction to Tom Eldridge.

Asking her friends' advice about Tom's proposal would have to wait. Today, she had a more important mission.

The excited buzz of conversation around her was growing, and Lili wondered if the situation was getting out of hand. The last thing she wanted was for the building's management to close the door to any type of negotiation.

"Hi, Lili!" Rita walked up with her lunch tray. "Your message sounded important. What's up?"

"Several things," Lili said, trying to ignore the raised voices around her. To add to her unease, someone at a nearby table was taking bets as to what would happen when the culprit was found. Another voice proposed taking up a collection in support of that person. If she hadn't already known she had to do something to calm the situation, Lili knew it now.

She also had to do something about Rita.

"First of all," Lili stated in an undertone, "I know I asked you and April to help me try to keep the center open. It's just that one or both of you went too far."

Rita, by now having caught the drift of the conversations around them, nodded cautiously as she picked up her sandwich. "Yeah, I heard something about the plane. So?"

"Well," Lili continued, glancing around to make sure

they weren't being overheard, "I think the person who hired the plane had to be you."

Rita paused in midbite. "Say again?"

Lili wasn't going to take that as a denial, no matter how innocent her friend tried to look. "If you'd been at the picnic yesterday, you'd know what I'm talking about."

"Sounds cool. Sorry I missed it. Actually, I was home enjoying being a new bride. Colby and I are still honeymooning." Rita grinned and went back to her lunch.

Lili wasn't fooled. Rita might have been at home yesterday, but it didn't require a genius to know that all it would have taken to finance the stunt was a telephone call and a credit card number. Furthermore, knowing Rita's carefree approach to life—"why not?" instead of "why?"—she was the perfect candidate to have come up with the attention-getting idea.

The unlikely marriage between Rita, a breezy research librarian, and Colby, a serious former Texas Ranger, proved that opposites attract, Lili thought wistfully. It should have been a source of comfort to herself. As it was, Tom had hardly noticed her until the other day at the picnic. If Paulette hadn't wildly kicked that soccer ball, with unfortunate results, he might not have noticed her at all.

Tom was likely upstairs in his office right now, trying to find out who had paid for yesterday's protest. He was probably planning on giving two weeks' notice and a severance check as soon as he found the person.

April was waltzing across the crowded lunchroom. "Sorry I'm late, Lili," she said breathlessly as she approached their table and sat down. "I only have a few minutes—I can't stay for lunch. But you sounded so serious when you called that I had to come down and find out what's up. Something happen?"

"Plenty," Lili answered. "I'm sure you've heard about the airplane flyover yesterday?"

April nodded.

"Tom is not only angry over what happened yesterday at the picnic, I think he's ready to fire whoever planned it."

Out of the corner of her eye, Lili saw Rita blanch at the word *fire* and put down her sandwich. If Lili hadn't been sure Rita was behind the stunt, she was now. Rita might be a wild card, but at least she was an honest one.

April shook her head. "Sorry, Lili. I don't have a clue what you're talking about, but it wasn't me. How about telling me what happened yesterday in one simple sentence before I have to get back upstairs? Did someone get hurt at the picnic?"

"Yes and no," Lili answered. She decided to keep Tom's injury to herself, in case Rita came up with one of her X-rated remarks. She rubbed her aching forehead and told April about the airplane towing a banner protesting the closure of the day care center.

"I know I asked you two for help," she added with a pointed look at Rita, "but the results were amazing."

"Cool!" April grinned wickedly. "Knowing how Tom reacts when he thinks he's lost control, I wish I'd been there to see him in action. But it wasn't me, Lili, I swear. Lucas and I were at the university lab going over the results of his new questionnaires on the mating game. By the way," she chirped happily, "now that I've shown Lucas that all women aren't alike, you'll be glad to know he's going to revise those six rules of his."

Even as Lili nodded, her gaze swung back to Rita.

After a pregnant moment, her friend shoved her sandwich away and nodded reluctantly. "Yeah, I guess it's time for the truth. I was only trying to help."

April shook her head. "Some help you were. From what I've heard, it sounds as if you've managed to turn the Riverview into a war zone. If you don't get us all fired, it's going to be a miracle."

Rita looked alarmed. "Heck, I was only trying to help. I thought a banner flying over the park would reach a lot more people than any fliers would. I didn't have a clue anyone would get their shorts tied in a knot over it."

"Unfortunately, someone has," Lili informed her. "How could you afford to pay for the airplane, anyway? And what did Colby say when he heard what you planned?"

Rita grinned smugly. "He thought it was a great idea. As for how much it cost, the pilot is a friend of Colby's. All I had to pay for was the banner—fifty bucks. I figured it was a lot cheaper than having fliers made up, and a lot more fun." Rita paused. "Are you going to tell Tom? Do you really think he'll fire me if he finds out I was the one who arranged for the plane?"

Lili reached into her purse and took out a bottle of pain relievers to soften the throbbing headache she'd had all day. Popping two tablets into her mouth, she reached for Rita's lemonade and took a sip. "No, I'm not going to tell him it was you. And yes, he'll probably fire you if he finds out for sure you did it. But only because the building's owner happened to see the banner."

"No way," April interjected. "I've known Tom for

years. He's too loyal to his employees to want to fire anyone. I'm sure he'll think of some way to get around it."

Rita muttered into her sandwich.

"Well, as my grandmother used to say, 'what is done is done,'" Lili said at last. "Now we must try to find a way to take care of the other problems before it is too late."

Rita blinked. "Other problems? What other problems? Besides my getting fired for trying to do something constructive, what other problems can there be?"

"Tom told me the building's owner will have to eventually raise the tenants' rents when the leases come due if he has to keep the center open. From what Tom said, some tenants might have to relocate in that case."

"Then it's up to us to come up with an idea to help Tom change the owner's mind." April jumped to her feet. "I have to get back to work, but give me a day or two. I'll talk it over with Lucas. Maybe he can come up with something."

"I'm really sorry," Rita said contritely after April left. "I had no idea the management would become so angry."

"Neither did I." Lili sighed. "I'm not sure Tom will be happy if we try to help him, but April is right. We have to find another way to save the center."

Rita's eyes lit up. "I know! We can sell cookies! You know, like the Girl Scout cookie drive!"

"That would take too many cookies!" Lili put her fingers to her lips and motioned toward a neighboring table, where a woman had just bet fifty dollars that the person behind the airplane flyover would be found and fired before the week was out.

"Oh, I don't know," Rita answered. "We sold cookies to raise funds in high school, and my folks used to say they practically paid for the lights in the football stadium with all the boxes they helped me sell. If that's not good enough," she added when Lili didn't look amused, "I'll talk it over with Colby. He knows a lot of well-placed people here in Chicago. Maybe he has an idea where we can find a fairy godfather."

"Not before you tell me what you're planning before you do it," Lili said, almost afraid to encourage Rita. Heaven only knew what she might come up with. Lili rose to leave.

"Hey, wait a minute. You haven't had any lunch!"

"No, I wasn't hungry." Lili rubbed her aching forehead. "I have a peanut butter and jelly sandwich upstairs in the studio waiting for me." She wasn't going to tell her friend she was on a strict budget so she could keep the twins in the center.

She blew Rita an air kiss and hurried to the elevators. She'd planned on telling her friends about pretending to be Tom's date at dinner on Friday, but had changed her mind. Recalling the way Rita's eyes lit up whenever Lili mentioned Tom, she was afraid that any date with him, real or not, might wind up another fiasco.

Besides, she thought as she made her way to Tom's office, a woman like herself didn't need any advice about men. Knowing how to handle a man was every Frenchwoman's birthright.

Lili knocked on his open office door. "Is this a good time to talk to you?"

When Tom frowned, she turned to leave. "Perhaps later?"

"No, wait." Tom eyed Lili. Gone was the minuscule yellow sundress that had caught his interest at yesterday's picnic. Today, she was dressed in beige linen slacks and a soft sapphire blouse that matched her almond shaped eyes. A narrow brown leather belt encircled her tiny waist. Around her neck, she wore a simple gold chain, and at her ears, gold studs. If he'd had any doubt that he'd been head over heels in lust with Lili yesterday, even in the midst of a highly sensitive personal problem, those doubts were gone today.

Until he'd caught her drawing up those damn fliers, he'd thought of Lili as a "Sullivan woman," demure and retiring. He knew better now. "What is it?"

"I came to see if you feel a little better after what happened yesterday," she replied with a charming blush that sent Tom's libido stirring. Not for the first time, he wondered how he could be so attracted to a woman who had created so much turmoil in his life.

Tom waved Lili into the office. "If you mean the soccer ball, yeah. If you're talking about the airplane stunt with the banner, the answer is no. In fact, I've just been on the phone with the company that owns the plane. No matter what I say, they claim customer privacy."

Lili murmured in sympathy. "Perhaps the incident is better forgotten?"

"I wish, but after yesterday, I think we both know better than that." Tom scowled at the phone and pushed it away as if it was to blame for the problem. "Dad cornered Kagan last night and called to tell me they've finally met and are talking. From what I gather, the stunt isn't going to be forgotten, at least for now. Kagan not only wants an apology, he wants the hide of whoever came up with the idea."

"You are sure?"

"Yeah," Tom answered with another jaundiced glance at the telephone. "I'm sure."

Lili blinked at the harsh terms of surrender. No way was she going to turn in Rita. Even an apology from the person who had hired the airplane wouldn't guarantee the center would be kept open. And working to keep it open for all the parents like herself who worked in the Riverview Building was something Lili felt she must continue to do. Life might not always be fair, as she'd often told the twins, but she'd never been one to give up without trying to somehow make it better.

Lili tried to concentrate on her crusade, but found herself thinking how sexy Tom looked as he ran his hand over his rugged chin. He proved the old saying that left-handed men were sexier than right-handed men, she thought wistfully.

As for the possibility that he could have an interest in her... Judging from the frustrated look on his face, the answer was no.

But she'd think about that later. It was time to try to calm the troubled waters.

Folding her hands in her lap demurely, Lili smiled at him. "I came to tell you that I have made up my mind. I will be pleased to be your date at your father's dinner Friday night."

To her surprise, Tom didn't look as happy as she thought he would. "But first," she added, before he could turn her down, "I would like to know why your father feels it is important for you to marry now. You are still young."

Tom frowned. His marital status was no one's business but his own. But there was no way he wanted anyone to think he was afraid of his father. Certainly not Lili.

He knew from personnel records that his father had a heart murmur, and Tom figured the condition must have played a part in Homer's early retirement. But Homer kept complaining he didn't have enough to do to keep him busy, and threatened to return to work. No way would Tom jeopardize his father's health by letting that happen. Nor did he want his dad to know he knew about his medical condition.

He settled for a half-truth. "Since you asked… First, my father wants to make sure I have a son to pass the magazine on to, just as he did with me. Secondly, he's determined to become a grandfather."

Lili nodded politely. "I think your father is a wise man."

Tom snorted. "That's your take. Mine is that my dad is a conniving if lovable man. If he wasn't, I wouldn't be sitting here now."

Lili wanted to know just where Tom would rather be, but was afraid to ask.

Tom waited for Lili, who didn't seem to miss a beat, to comment. When she smiled, he went on. "Now that my life is an open book, something tells me there's a catch to your offer. Right?"

Prepared to stand her ground no matter how intimidating Tom became, Lili smiled demurely. "Yes. I have decided to, as you say, make a deal with you."

Tom laughed. "I knew it! Somewhere in that busy mind of yours, there had to be a catch. Otherwise, you wouldn't have come up with the idea of humoring my father in the first place. Go ahead, spit it out."

"It is only this. If you help your father persuade this

Mr. Kagan to forget yesterday's airplane flyover and allow us to raise money for the day care center, I will pretend to be your date."

Tom's eyebrows rose. "I have a feeling there's more to this bargain."

"Yes. I will be your pretend date not only for this dinner, but until you have no further need to keep your father happy."

Tom managed to smother a snort. Only an unsophisticated woman would have come up with such an offer. Any modern American woman would realize that proximity, pretend or not, had its rewards. Rewards Lili obviously wasn't anticipating.

If she wasn't a widow with small children, Tom would have thought she'd never heard of the birds and the bees. Pretend to be his date for the foreseeable future? Did she think he was a man of iron?

If Lili only knew how he felt about her.

"No deal," he said. "Although I'm not saying I don't want to help your crusade. I will if I find a way to do so. The problem is that it's not only up to me. There are dozens of tenants in the building and they're all in the same boat with their leases. None of us want higher rents. Like I keep telling you, closing the center is simply a matter of good business."

"It is also good business to allow women with children to work," Lili retorted. "And a safe and healthy environment is good for children."

"Sure," Tom agreed, "but there are other considerations in tough economic times. The day care center has grown so much it can no longer be run as a nonprofit enterprise. It's become a business. And from what I've heard, an unsuccessful one."

Lili nodded reluctantly. There was no way she was going to tell Tom she was planning to raise the needed funds without antagonizing the building's owner any further.

"Let's face it, Lili. Providing a day care at Riverview has lost its appeal for Kagan."

"Does that mean your answer to my proposition is no? You do not want me to be your date?"

Tom hesitated. He wasn't too sure about the wisdom of asking Lili to pretend to be his love interest, but he couldn't bring himself to say no. After all, she'd been the one to suggest it be for more than one night. Unless... From the expression on Lili's face, there had to be more to her proposition than she'd shared with him.

"Maybe," he said at last. "But I have to know what you want in exchange for the charade."

"First, you must help your father persuade Mr. Kagan to keep an open mind about keeping the center running."

Tom had a feeling Kagan wasn't going to be easy to persuade. "And then?"

She smiled. "And then you must help me find a way to raise money for the center."

Tom weighed Lili's offer. What she was "suggesting" was nothing less than blackmail, even if it was delivered with a smile. For a shy woman, she was turning out to be made of steel.

Damned if he didn't have to admire her for that.

After rescuing his magazine from the brink of bankruptcy, Tom knew more than he'd ever wanted to know about red ink. Thanks to publishing "Sullivan's Rules," the magazine was in the black now.

If he set his mind to it, finding a way to finance Lili's

crusade shouldn't turn out to be too difficult. All he wanted to do was keep his father healthy and happy.

But asking Tom to forget firing the mastermind behind the airplane stunt was another thing, especially now that he knew it wasn't Lili. But considering it was Lili doing the asking, maybe it wasn't too high a price to pay.

Being seen with her was another problem. In spite of his policy not to fraternize with members of his staff, she was growing on him.

"Okay," he finally agreed. "I'll try to come up with an idea to raise money for the center. But—"

"Coffee, tea, cold drinks?" Arthur appeared in the doorway. "In case either of you has been too busy to go for lunch, I have turkey sandwiches."

Tom mentally blessed Arthur for the interruption. A break for lunch would give him time to pretend he wasn't giving in to Lili too easily. Who knew what condition of surrender she might come up with the next time they bumped heads if he did?

"Lili? How about a sandwich?"

To his relief, she accepted the sandwich and a cold drink. After taking a sandwich for himself, he sat back and studied the serene expression on her face.

He might not have decided to take Lili up on her offer, but considering he was beginning to know how her mind worked, it looked as if she believed he'd already agreed to her bargain.

What surprised him even more was the pleasure he felt at the prospect of having Lili as a date for the foreseeable future.

As for Kagan, unless Homer asked for help in trying to persuade the guy to turn a blind eye to what Lili and her friends were up to, Tom intended to leave the man to his father. It would keep his dad too busy to worry about Tom's marital future.

What he had to do, Tom realized, was find a fairy godfather with a bundle of money to keep the center open. And, heaven help him, avoid falling for Lili.

Or was it already too late?

Chapter Five

On Tuesday, Tom decided that no matter how reluctant he was to get involved in Lili's crusade, it was high time to visit the child care center.

He hoped Lili understood that he wasn't against either her or her crusade. His previous lack of enthusiasm had been largely because he knew zip about children or a day care center, let alone what it cost to run one. The truth was, as a businessman, he had been more interested in balance sheets than in the children themselves.

Except that things had changed. Last Sunday, Lili had made him see children as children instead of dollar signs.

The other truth was that he'd finally realized he wanted Lili in all the ways a man wanted a desirable woman.

As proof of his attraction to Lili, her bizarre suggestion that they appear to date for the foreseeable future was actually beginning to make sense.

Normally a pragmatic man, he'd agreed to Lili's terms. Originally he'd believed a convenient "romance" was a good idea—under ordinary circumstances. The problem was that these were no longer ordinary circumstances.

He had a magazine to run, a determined father to protect from himself, and now, of all the unlikely possibilities, a child care center to save. If there was any way to fulfill the bargain he'd made with Lili, he had to concentrate on dollar signs instead of a pair of sparkling blue eyes.

He reminded himself that he'd done the impossible before by putting *Today's World* on its financial feet. If he could just manage to put himself heart and soul into Lili's project, he should be able to do it again.

Deep in thought, he pushed the elevator down button. Turning *Today's World* into a widely read magazine hadn't been easy, and Lucas's article had been a critical component of that success.

Too bad his friend hadn't come up with a few rules about raising kids, Tom mused as he waited for the elevator to reach the basement. A how-to article on the subject could very well start another reader riot. By the time the dust settled, he could donate a percentage of the resulting revenue to fund a portion of the center's expenses.

Until he could persuade Lucas to at least consider writing an article about kids, Tom had no choice but to seek other avenues of help. He'd made a bargain with Lili, and in order to keep his end of it, he had to check out the center and find out what he was up against. The trick was to tackle the financial problems of the day care just as he would any other business venture.

The elevator stopped to pick up new passengers, and all became quickly engaged in a discussion about the threatened closure. During the time it took to reach the basement, Tom realized he'd underestimated the depth and scope of Lili's undercover activities. It sounded as if the Riverview's entire population was up in arms.

To add to his unease, he suddenly realized there was something missing from the agreement he'd made with Lili.

He'd forgotten to get Lili's promise to cease and desist from pursuing activities that antagonized the building's owner.

Tom also had an uneasy feeling that while he was keeping his part of their bargain, Lili was probably upstairs in the magazine's art studio hatching up another plan or two.

If only he hadn't allowed her Gallic charm to muddle his thinking.

Not soon enough for him, the elevator door slid open in front of the cafeteria. He noticed Lili standing in the coffee line. He also caught sight of several of her inflammatory fliers pinned to the community bulletin board just inside the cafeteria door. A group of employees was standing in front of the board in heated debate over whether to start a strike to get management's attention.

As if Lili hadn't stirred enough excitement over the issue already.

The amount of money that would be lost by both the business owners and employees in the event of a building-wide strike boggled his mind. It was time for action. A saner mind had to step in.

Since Lili had chosen Tom to become the center's savior, Riverview's problems had become his.

Muttering to himself, Tom avoided eye contact with Lili and backed out of the cafeteria. Hoping for the best, he strode down the hall and pushed open a door marked Care Center. He found himself in a small, enclosed foyer in front of another door with a digital security mechanism he hadn't a clue how to operate. It looked as if knocking the old-fashioned way was the only chance he had to get inside.

Before he could raise his hand, a warning bell above his head went off. The door opened, and an elderly white-haired woman stepped out to confront him. Her badge identified her simply as Mary, but from the steely look in her eyes, she could have been named Goliath.

"Yes?"

Tom pointed to his identification badge before he remembered he wasn't wearing it. Still, he'd never been denied entry anywhere in the building before.

He searched in his back pocket for his wallet, drew out a business card that identified him as the owner and publisher of *Today's World*, and handed it over. "Good morning, ma'am. I'm Tom Eldridge."

The woman slowly surveyed him from the top of his head to his highly polished shoes, and he stirred uneasily. When her gaze stopped at his shoes, he glanced down to make sure they matched.

"Sorry, young man," she said as she handed him back the card. "I'm afraid I don't recognize you as having a child staying with us."

Tom understood from the firm set of the woman's lips and the cell phone in her hand that she meant business and was ready to call security. If he couldn't come up with a believable story, and fast, he'd be back in the elevator, or worse yet, in custody.

He tried a winning smile. "No, I'm sorry, Mary…?" He cocked his head in inquiry.

"London, Mary London," she offered, but the look in her eyes didn't soften.

"Mrs. London," Tom continued, "you're right. I have

no children in your care. That is," he added when her eyes narrowed, "I have employees who do. I was asked to check out the center on their behalf."

The woman hesitated. "If this is a security inspection, Mr. Eldridge, I can assure you no one gets through this door unless they know the combination. Which—" her voice took on an icy edge "—you don't. You can report that little item to whoever sent you. So, unless you have another reason for being here, or unless you leave now, I'm afraid..." Her voice trailed off, but her message was clear. She was ready to call for help.

Tom mentally explored the possibilities of talking his way inside the day care without attracting the attention of the very people he was trying to avoid. No way did he want to antagonize the building's management. He might need their help someday.

His mind whirled at the awkwardness of the situation. Without any children at the day care, he had no reason being there. No wonder Mrs. London was barring his entry. Still...since Lili *was* the reason he was here in the first place, maybe mentioning her name would be the magic formula to get him inside.

"Lili Soulé, an employee of mine, asked me to stop by and see if I could be of help."

"The Lili Soulé whose children are in after-school care?"

Tom nodded.

Without taking her eyes off him, the keeper of the door whipped out her cell phone and punched in a number. From unhappy personal experience, Tom guessed that the exuberance and curiosity of the Soulé twins probably required more than one call to their mother.

Otherwise he would have been surprised the woman knew Lili's telephone number by heart.

Three minutes later, he was standing at the entrance to a large room, where twelve pairs of curious eyes regarded him solemnly.

The children were seated at low, brightly colored tables for some kind of snack break, it seemed. Twelve upper lips were covered with milk mustaches. Twelve pairs of hands held chocolate chip cookies minus a bite or two. Paper napkins, intended to keep those small lips clean, were scattered on the floor.

He nodded and checked out the rest of the area. Picture books filled bookcases. Children's artwork was pinned to one wall with colored tape, a bright alphabet poster on another. Green plants and small flower arrangements were scattered on top of the bookcases. A cage on a shelf contained a rabbit busily gnawing on a carrot. The animal's intense chewing sounds seemed to match Tom's own nervous internal rhythm.

A few younger children were sleeping curled up on cots in the far corner, and through an open door, he spotted a pristine kitchen where a woman dressed in white was busily chopping fresh vegetables and dropping them into a steaming pot. Lunch?

But what really drew Tom's attention was a small boy standing in front of a paper-covered easel, drawing a series of trees. That could have been him at the same age, Tom mused, as Mrs. London's attention was diverted by the telephone.

He'd been hooked on art from the day his mother first put a crayon in his hand. Nurtured by his mother, who'd had a minor success as an artist, he'd even planned on going to a prestigious art institute when he grew up—until his father had started the magazine. The day Homer had announced he intended to create a publishing dynasty, with Tom waiting in the wings to take over, had signaled the end of Tom's dreams to be an artist.

A master's degree in business with a minor in journalism had resulted, but Tom's interest in art had never waned, just gone underground.

"Nice tree," he said to the boy, whose interest in art apparently was greater than his interest in cookies. "What kind of tree is it?"

"A pumpkin tree." The boy reached for an orange crayon.

Tom didn't have the heart to tell the kid pumpkins didn't grow on trees. He looked too happy adding the orange globes here and there among the green foliage for Tom to disillusion him.

"Like pumpkins, do you?"

The boy nodded solemnly. "Yeah. My mother makes the best pumpkin pies in the whole world."

"I like pumpkin pie, too," Tom answered. "They're my favorite. By the way, how many trees do you intend to draw?"

"A whole orchard, so we can have lots of pumpkins." The boy drew a bright yellow sun above the tree. "To make the pumpkins grow," he explained as he drew another sun.

Tom nodded solemnly. "Good thinking. By the way, my name's Tom. What's yours?"

When the boy glanced at Mrs. London for approval, Tom knew he shouldn't have asked the question. He should have remembered today's children were raised never to speak to strangers.

Tom smiled. "See you around."

He wandered back to Mary London. Whatever Lili had told her on the phone seemed to have worked. This time, the lady greeted him with a smile.

"Now, what can I do for you?" she asked, gesturing to a group of chairs in the corner. "Let's go sit down and we'll talk."

Sit down? Tom eyed the small chairs warily before he sighed and folded himself in to a pretzel, his chin almost meeting his knees. "Are these all the children you have in day care?"

"My stars, no," Mary answered with a laugh, and gestured to an adjoining room. "It's story time for some of the older children, and we have an infant program. As for these, it's nap time, you know," she added fondly. "We pride ourselves on keeping our children on a healthy schedule."

Tom didn't know beans about babies, but he did know that parents paid only a nominal fee to keep their children here. The center was too small to be self-supporting, especially when he estimated the costs of employing the two young women who were monitoring the kids at break time. Even if they were college students, they had to be working for minimum wage. Then there was the woman in the kitchen, and another Tom had glimpsed walking by with a load of fresh linen.

He mentally added the services of a nurse and possibly the on-call services of one of the doctors with an office in the building. Then there was Mary London's salary.

Even if he included the children who would be showing up for afternoon care, it was clear there wasn't enough income generated to have the center break even.

No wonder Kagan, an internationally known business-man, had decided to throw in the towel.

For Lili's sake, Tom tried to be positive, even hope-ful. Still, no businessman worth his salary would ignore the center's balance sheets. Furthermore, by continuing to circulate petitions and create inflammatory fliers, Lili was making his job difficult, if not impossible.

If only he'd remembered to get her promise to cease stirring the already boiling pot. At least long enough to give him a chance to come up with a game plan to help.

The thought brought him back to Mrs. London's change of attitude. "I'm pretty sure Lili told you why I'm here. Right?"

"Right," she agreed with a smile. "Now, just what can I do for you—other than showing you around?"

"I would like to begin by looking at your books."

Mrs. London shook her head. "Oh dear, I was afraid you might ask. Actually, I can't, even if I wanted to. All our records are kept upstairs in the building's manage-ment office."

Tom fought off the temptation to groan.

"I'm sorry, Mrs. London," he said. "Under the cir-cumstances, short of breaking and entering to look at those balance sheets, I'm not sure what I can do to help you."

"Oh dear!" Mrs. London repeated nervously as the children finished their snack and got up from their ta-bles. With a murmured apology, she motioned for an aide to take charge. "I would never ask you to do any-thing against the law."

"I know," Tom said. "I'll just tell Lili you tried to help. There has to be some other way."

"That's what I'm trying to tell you, Mr. Eldridge," Mrs. London said. "I may not be very knowledgeable about finances, but I'm sure we can find something for you to do around here—something to give you an idea of what we're up against. As a businessman, you can always translate what problems you see into dollars, can't you?"

Tom regarded the woman warily. How could he refuse her request for help? He was about to get an education in what it took to care for children. He forced a smile as he glanced at the messy snack table. If only he could be educated without getting smeared with melted marshmallows or paint.

As for Mary London, a woman who professed to know little about business, she was doing just fine manipulating him. The look in her eyes told him she intended to take full advantage of him.

"Just what did you have in mind?" he asked.

"We need more books," she said brightly. "You might not believe it, but a few of the little ones are already learning to read from the posters and pictures we have on the walls."

Tom nodded cautiously. "That's it?"

"We also need someone to be here for a few hours every day to help the children with their reading."

Tom's heart sank. Children's books he was ready to supply, but from the sparkle in Mrs. London's eyes, he was sure that wasn't all she had in mind. She might want hands-on help with reading to the kids, but that help wasn't going to come from him.

"If you want me to teach children to read," Tom said, trying to keep the horror from his voice, "I'm afraid you've got the wrong guy."

Mrs. London beamed as if she'd just won a lottery. "You certainly are quick, young man. Of course I do."

"Not me," Tom protested. "From what I can remember of my own experience, teaching someone to read takes special skill. Maybe I can find some of my employees who might want to volunteer. I have a magazine to run."

"I wouldn't ask," she answered briskly, "except that I'm in a desperate situation here. An hour a day of your time—or that of someone from your office—would definitely help until you find a way for us to fund a teacher. Or…" she glanced across the room "…maybe someone who can work with our Tommy a few hours a week." She nodded at the little boy busily painting pumpkin trees. "Tommy displays a positive gift for art, don't you think?"

"Tommy?" The kid had already touched him with his love of art. Had Mrs. London sensed that Tom himself was a closet artist?

"Well," he said reluctantly, "I guess I could find some time to drop in now and then to help out with Tommy. As for the rest, I'll have to do some research in order to calculate the cost of hiring a teacher with the proper credentials to work with the children."

The only bright spot on the horizon was the possibility of being able to coax some of his staff to volunteer their services. Maybe, he thought with a wry stab of pleasure, since Homer seemed so fond of small children, Tom could draft his father.

Any way he looked at it, the dollar signs were adding up faster than he could count. He began to have sympathy for Kagan.

Just as he was about to ask if Mrs. London had anything else to say to him, Lili appeared in the doorway, smiled and headed toward him. Behind her, he caught a glimpse of the twins pushing their way into the center.

"Early, aren't you?" Tom glanced at his watch and slowly rose from his cramped position on the small chair, keeping a cautious eye on Paulette. "Is something wrong with one of the twins?"

Lili looked puzzled. "No. The twins' school closes early on Tuesdays. I pick them up and bring them here on my lunch hour." Clearly worried by his question, she asked, "Is there a problem?"

Before he could answer, Paulette headed for a large rubber ball and picked it up. With a whoop, she began to bounce it.

Instinctively, Tom ducked. When the ball bounced past him, he breathed a sigh of relief. "If you thought that bringing the kids would help to convince me the center's survival is critical, you didn't have to bother. I told you I'd try to help."

Lili smiled. "Thank you."

What Tom didn't add was that after his discussion with Mrs. London, it was clear it would take more than his help to get the center on a firm financial footing. It would take a blooming miracle.

At the moment, he already had more problems on his plate than he had time to worry about. The day care's financial future was the least of them.

He had the magazine to run.

He had to find a way to keep a watchful eye on Lili so she would stay out of trouble.

He had to prevent his father from scheming to bring him and Lili together in the bonds of matrimony.

And there was Lili herself—an impossibly charming woman who seemed to contradict every one of Sullivan's Rules.

"Like I said, I'll try." Tom edged away from her tantalizing scent. If he stayed here any longer, he'd start picturing her in his arms. Who knew what she might get him to promise if that ever happened?

"I'm sorry, I have to go back to the office," he said. "I've been gone too long as it is."

"Oh, Mr. Eldridge! About those hours for Tommy?" Mary London called after him.

"I'll be back," Tom answered her, striding to the door before the motherly director could stop him.

"Motherly, like hell," he muttered under his breath as he let himself out the security door. Beneath her tidy white hair and genteel appearance, Mary London was a strong woman like Lili. One way or another, women were trying to take over his life.

Lili gazed thoughtfully after Tom. "Time? For what, Mary?"

The older woman hesitated. "Perhaps you should ask Mr. Eldridge, dear. I don't feel right discussing any plans he and I spoke about until they actually happen. It's just not lucky. But I can tell you that when it comes to your Mr. Eldridge, I have high hopes for him."

Lili managed a smile. *Her* Mr. Eldridge? If only Mrs. London knew that at one time Lili had had high hopes for herself and Tom. She knew better now.

Her offer to act as Tom's date for the foreseeable future was not, as her friend April had maintained in discussions of the mating game, simply a question of searching for a potential mate with strong genes. Although, Lili thought with a wry grin as she went looking for her small son, Tom appeared to have more than enough of them.

Nor was the way she felt about him merely a case of a natural and normal sexual attraction, as her friend

Rita might have suggested before she'd married Colby Callahan.

The truth was that while Tom might not be the most handsome man Lili had ever met, he was, in her own mind at least, the most intelligent and the most interesting.

She might be on the verge of losing her heart to Tom, but considering the way he felt about marriage and children, he was the last man she should have chosen.

Chapter Six

Marriage was all well and good, Tom reasoned, as long as it didn't include him.

He'd come close to losing his single status with an I'm-going-to-do-it-my-way classmate when he'd been a senior in college, and the unpleasant experience still rankled. He'd been wary of strong and independent women ever since.

So why was he thinking of marriage more often these days, and why did those thoughts include Lili? His only concern should be the ongoing challenge of keeping his magazine profitable, and in order to do that, he had to keep Lili from further antagonizing Riverview's management.

He reached across his desk for the copy of *Today's World* that featured "Sullivan's Rules." Maybe a guy like him needed to reread the six rules every so often to put his physical attraction to Lili in perspective.

Rule Number three, "A woman must rein in her own desires to promote the health of a relationship." That seemed to cover his Lili problem. Not that he had a real relationship with her, he thought with an unexpected pang of disappointment.

Rule Number five, "A woman must show her man how much she likes and appreciates him. She must shower him with affection and sublimate her own daily frustrations."

Clearly, Lili was not willing to ignore her frustrations with the day care problem even if it caused him grief.

Tom closed the magazine. His original attraction to Lili had been on a physical level, but now he had to admit to a grudging admiration for her dedication to her crusade.

Thoughts of Lili were abruptly cut off as the door to Tom's office opened.

"Speak of the devil," he remarked dryly when Lucas Sullivan, the author of "Sullivan's Rules," strode in.

Lucas dropped into a chair. "And to think April told me you actually wanted to see me. What's the matter, Tom? You look as if you've just been bitten by a snake."

"I think I've been had by the oldest snake in the book," Tom agreed, "but that's another story." He gestured to the magazine with Sullivan's article on the cover. "I wanted to ask you to write another piece for us. But first I've got to know—do you still believe these rules?"

Lucas glanced at the magazine cover. "I wrote that shortly before I met and married April. As for believing in them now, I'm not so sure. I'm actually working on updating my survey."

"What's the subject going to be?"

Lucas grinned. "Women."

"Yeah? I thought that's what 'Sullivan's Rules' was all about."

"According to April, women want to play an equal role in the mating game. And, heaven help me—" Lucas shrugged "—she's made me see the light."

"That's a hell of a change," Tom said, scowling.

"I take it you're having a problem with a woman. Who's the lucky lady?"

"Unfortunately, it's Lili Soulé, the magazine's graphic artist," Tom muttered. "You wouldn't believe the uproar she's caused around here."

Lucas murmured in sympathy. "Ah yes, April's told me about Lili's crusade. If you're interested in Lili on a personal level, you'll forget any of the baggage that comes with her and concentrate on the woman underneath."

Tom sat back in his chair. "This is about more than Lili's crusade. It also involves my father. For years he's been after me to settle down, marry and provide him with grandchildren. This time he has his sights on Lili, who, by the way, comes with six-year-old twins, a boy and a girl."

"You have something against kids?"

Tom repressed a shudder. "No—not really. That is, you'd have to know these two kids to understand how I feel. The girl is as headstrong as her mother—something I had to learn the hard way."

Lucas chuckled when Tom told him about the employees' picnic and getting hit with a soccer ball.

"The kid's a menace," Tom said. "I can just tell. I'm afraid I'll wind up being her target."

"And the boy?"

Tom related the story of Paul's encounter with the gopher. "He seems harmless enough, I know. But I'm not sure I can cope with the kid's intellectual curiosity. From the look in his eyes, I have this feeling he's a ticking time bomb."

"Sounds like an intelligent kid," Lucas said. "I'd say

the real problem is coming to terms with whatever's going on between you and his mother. If you can sort that out, the children should be doable. My advice is to just give it time."

"Time," Tom grumbled. "That's part of the problem. I have the sinking feeling I'm running out of time!"

"Whoa—you've got it bad. Either you're infatuated with Lili, or you're actually falling in love with her. Either way, it sounds as if you're going to have to make up your mind about her or get out of her way."

"Easier said than done." Tom's thoughts turned to sexy legs and rosy lips and intelligent flashing eyes. Even her accent managed to charm the socks off him. "There's no way I can get out of Lili's way, even if I tried. Her crusade is not only affecting my business, it's affecting me. I can't stop thinking about her."

"You're complaining?"

"Being attracted to Lili isn't the whole problem," Tom admitted. "And it's not the children, either. I'm old enough to remember that most infatuations are nothing more than stirred up testosterone that can leave a guy not knowing his own name. Real love, on the other hand…"

"…makes a guy feel like a real man." Lucas finished the sentence for him. "You're on target. Only you're not sure you're ready for a commitment. Right?"

"Yeah," Tom agreed. "That's part of the problem. At thirty-eight, I'm too old to become a father."

"No way! We're the same age, you know. Personally, just as soon as April's ready, I'm looking forward to hearing the patter of little feet."

"Not me, not yet," Tom said fervently.

Lucas laughed. "The way I see it, you've thought a

lot about the mating game and you're afraid of the answers you've come up with. I don't think you need any additional advice on the subject from me. I'm sure you'll have the right answers when the time comes."

Tom forced his thoughts away from Lili and back to the reason he'd asked Lucas to drop by. "Actually, I called you here because I want you to write another article for *Today's World.* Something about kids. The magazine could use another shot in the arm."

"Wait a few years." Lucas grinned. "Right now, I know less about kids than I do about women."

"Yeah, but look at it this way. Your article 'Sullivan's Rules' sold a lot of magazines. I figure that if you could write a piece that would send our circulation through the roof again, I'd be able to make a sizable donation to the building's child care center and make Lili happy at the same time."

Lucas declined with a laugh. "Sorry. You want to get me tarred and feathered for real instead of in the newspapers and on television?"

Tom's spirits sank. Unless he could come up with enough money to keep the center open, at least for a while, Lili was bound to be busy fighting windmills. "Nope. I just thought if you did write something about relationships that included children, it would help solve a problem."

"You've got to lighten up, Tom," Lucas said as he rose to leave. "Starting now. If you're not too busy, how about joining me for a beer? We can talk about the good old fraternity times we had back at Northwestern."

With a last rueful glance at the magazine, Tom agreed. "Might as well. I'm already in a hell of a mess. I don't know how things could get any worse."

AT SIX-THIRTY ON FRIDAY, Tom slowly drove through Chicago's North Side. He figured the sooner he picked up Lili and the twins and took them to his father's condo, the sooner he would be able to take them home.

It was the dinner in between that worried him.

As he drove away from the lake, two-story apartment houses and small brick suburban homes with front porches began to appear, reminding him of the neighborhood he'd lived in during his childhood.

That was before his father had purchased *Today's World* and set out to make a name for himself. The family had moved into a high-rise condo in one of the wealthier parts of Chicago.

Tom's life hadn't been the same since.

In Lili's neighborhood, people were strolling along the streets or hanging around front yards, talking. Children and dogs were chasing each other down the sidewalks. Scents of cooking filled the air.

He pulled up at the address Lili had given him. After a second glance, he realized he could have picked out the house even if she hadn't given him the number.

A wooden swing hung from the porch ceiling. Honeysuckle vines curved around the railings, intertwined with blue morning glories. A riot of colorful flowers framed the steps, and a beautiful welcome wreath of dried fruit hung on the door.

As Tom strode up the stairs, he realized there was more to Lili than met the eye. She might have taken on the role of crusader, but it was obvious her soul was that of a homemaker and artist.

Paulette answered the door at his third ring. Tom took a step backward. The kid might look like a miniature charmer in her go-to-dinner clothing, but she was staring at him with a lopsided scowl. Why did she have such an attitude with him? He'd been the injured party during their earlier encounter.

"Hi, remember me? I'm Tom Eldridge." He turned on a friendly smile. "I've come to take you to dinner." The girl's scowl grew deeper. "Something wrong?"

"Yeah. I want to stay home and play with my friends next door, but my mother won't let me. Who wants to go out to dinner with grown-ups!"

"You do." Lili's firm voice broke in as she appeared in the doorway and put her hands on Paulette's shoulders. "Now, go and find your brother and tell him to turn off his computer. It is time to leave."

"It sure sounds as if you had the right idea bringing the children to dinner tonight," Tom said wryly when Paulette grimaced and darted away. "I might have been dubious about the idea before, but not now. If Paulette turns off my father, we're home free."

Lili smiled and motioned him inside. "I'm afraid my daughter has a mind of her own. Come in, please. I am wrapping a gift for your father."

Tom followed her into the house. On the walls were several bright paintings of landscapes, and colorful rag rugs were scattered on the burnished pine floor. The furniture was a mix of overstuffed upholstered pieces and a rustic maple table and chairs. A mauve and pale green throw was tossed over the couch, games and toys littered the fireplace hearth, and the faint scent of baking filled the air.

And everything he saw seemed to reflect Lili's warm, passionate nature.

He wandered over to the fireplace mantel, where a photograph of a smiling man in uniform held a place of honor. Alongside it was a wedding picture of a smiling bride and groom, as well as small snapshots of the twins as babies, held by their smiling father. Since there were no later pictures of the family together, Tom guessed that Paul, Sr. had died soon after the twins' birth.

In spite of his earlier determination not to become emotionally involved with Lili, her past, present or future, Tom felt a tug at his heart. So much for being all business, he thought.

He turned away and glanced at the small dining room. The maple table was covered by a lace runner with red candles set in pewter holders. From the tiny kitchen beyond drifted the mouthwatering scent of freshly baked cookies, reminding Tom of his mother— before a cook had been hired. Chocolate chip cookies had never tasted the same after that.

Here was a home any sane man would be happy to call his own, Tom mused as he turned back to the living room. And Lili, the-oh-so charming, scheming Lili, was a woman a man would want to come home to.

His gaze strayed back to the smiling picture of her late husband. There seemed to be a challenge in the man's eyes and it was directed at Tom. Not only a challenge, a warning. If Tom was serious about Lili and the twins, the man's frank look said, he had better be prepared to take good care of them. To love them as he himself had loved them.

Tom returned the man's direct gaze. Lili's late husband had nothing to fear from him. After all, at her suggestion, he told himself righteously, he and Lili were only pretending to be a couple.

Still, the unspoken message was clear. Unless Tom intended to get serious about Lili, he should back off before it was too late.

He nodded in understanding. He intended to end this pretense with Lili, but not before he kept his promise. Within his capabilities, he would try to make at least one of her dreams come true: the survival of the child care center at Riverview.

As for her other dreams, Tom mused, Lili hadn't mentioned any of them to him. Even so, he knew she deserved a man who would work his heart out to make those dreams come true.

He just wasn't going to be that man.

"Tom? *Tom?*" Lili's voice broke into his reverie.

He shook off his thoughts. Lili was holding a small plastic container of cookies tied with a red ribbon. The twins were staring at him as if he had appeared from outer space.

"Yes?"

Her smile wavered. "Is something wrong? You have changed your mind about taking us to your father's for dinner?"

"Not at all." Tom tried to smother a sympathetic smile at the hopeful look in Paulette's eyes, but failed. He managed a wink instead, and got a frown in return.

He couldn't blame the kid. When she grew up, she would be just as determined and independent as her mother, he thought.

"I'm sorry," he said, aware of the three expectant faces before him. "I guess I was lost in thought." He strode to the front door and held it open. "My car is outside. Ready?"

For some reason Tom had an unshakable feeling that his life was about to change.

CONSIDERING PAULETTE'S usual gregarious nature until now, the silence during the ride to his father's condo was surprising, Tom thought. The glances he exchanged with Lili were not. It was obvious she was just as bewildered about the child's silence as he was.

Clearly, Lili was also puzzled at his own silence. For that matter, so was he.

Actually, it was lack of privacy that kept him from talking. He wanted to apologize for not being up front with Lili. He wanted to tell her that in spite of her offer to pretend to be his date, their bargain couldn't continue. He wasn't sure if he was ready for any kind of relationship, real or pretend.

If he hadn't read the message in her late husband's eyes, he would have felt less guilty. As it was, it had made him even more aware he could be falling for Lili.

A bad sign. Especially when she gave no indication how she really felt about him.

On the other hand, maybe he was reading something into the situation that wasn't actually there. Maybe all they had between them was a convenient arrangement, after all. An agreement they could break after his father's attention turned elsewhere.

And until Tom helped resolve the issue of the day care.

Tom's father greeted them at the door.

"Ah, at last!" Homer Eldridge said as he drew Lili inside. "And the children, too!" To Tom's jaundiced view, his father was beaming as if he'd won a lottery. "Come in. Come in. It's been too long since I heard children's voices in my home."

Tom bit back a wry comment. His workaholic father hadn't been at home long enough to hear the voices of

Tom or his sister. Heck, Megan was ten years younger than he was. She'd still been a child when Tom had left home for college. And knowing his sister, she had to have made a lot of noise.

No sooner had the irony of the situation hit him than his sister rushed through the kitchen door. She threw herself at Tom, hugging him fiercely. "Hi, big brother! Long time no see!"

Smiling at Megan's exuberance, Tom hugged her back. "Why didn't you let me know you were coming home?"

"I wanted to surprise you." Megan laughed happily as she eyed Tom's three companions. "I was visiting a friend in Los Angeles when I called Dad and he told me you were coming to dinner with a friend." She glanced over Tom's shoulder. "You didn't expect me to stay away when I heard the friend was a woman," she whispered. "I had to fly here and meet this *friend* for myself."

Tom felt himself flush as he introduced Lili and the twins. Megan was right. The one and only time he'd been naive enough to think he was in love, he hadn't gotten around to introducing the girl to his family. No wonder Megan had jumped at the chance to meet Lili.

Tom turned toward Lili now. "I'd like you to meet my sister, Megan. Megan, this is Lili Soulé. Lili works at the magazine as a graphic artist." He motioned to the twins, who were hanging back behind their mother. "And these two are her children, Paul and Paulette."

"Twins!" Megan crowed happily. "How lucky! Come on in before dinner gets cold."

"Yes, indeed." Homer Eldridge reached for the children's jackets. "Megan decided to give the cook the night off and make dinner herself tonight. She tells me she's made something special."

Something special turned out to be fresh lake white-fish, a local delicacy, mashed potatoes and a mixture of broccoli and carrots. From the look on the twins' faces, they weren't impressed. Tom wasn't impressed, either. Even *he* knew that kids would pass on fish. Unless, of course, it was fish sticks or fish and chips. And even then…

"How's the fish?" Megan asked when Paul stared glumly at his plate.

"Okay, I guess," the little boy said.

"Yeah," Paulette chimed in. "We like hamburgers and fries better."

"I only like fish when it's fish sticks," Paul complained.

Tom felt a pang of satisfaction. At least there was one thing he knew about kids.

Paulette stuck out her tongue at her brother. "You don't like fish sticks!"

"Do, too," he almost shouted.

Tom was about to intercede when he felt Lili nudge him in the ribs. The warning in her eyes told him not to interfere. He realized then that Lili had a plan. A plan to put his father off grandchildren.

"Please forgive them, Mr. Eldridge," she said quietly. "I know you said you were looking forward to hearing children's voices, but I'm afraid the children are not on their best behavior tonight."

Homer nodded and went back to eating. But not before he sent a calculating glance at the twins.

Tom bit back a sigh of relief. It looked as if Lili's plan was working.

"Mr. Eldridge, have you had a chance to speak to this Mr. Kagan about the center?"

Tom smothered a groan. The tenacious Lili hadn't been listening when he'd told her to leave the problem of the center to him.

"We're talking," Tom's father replied with a grimace. "Jules is a tough bird, but he hasn't heard the last from me."

"Thank you," Lili murmured. But from the look on her face, it was plain to Tom she still had plans of her own.

"Dessert, anyone?" Megan asked hopefully when it became evident the children were getting edgy.

Paul pushed his plate away. "What's for dessert?"

"Neapolitan ice cream and some of the cookies your mother brought."

The children still looked mutinous.

"Hold on a minute," Homer said. "Megan's gone to great lengths to please you children. The least you could do is try everything she's made."

Paulette clamped her lips shut.

Paul glared.

"No dinner, no dessert," Homer said firmly, much to Tom's surprise. He had expected his father to cater to the twins. "That's the way I raised my own children."

"That's okay," Paulette said. "I don't want dessert. Can we watch television?"

Homer frowned, then motioned them away. "Go ahead. Megan, why don't you bring ice cream and cookies for the rest of us. Lili?"

"No thank you." Lili rose from the table. "If you don't mind, I would like to check to make sure the children are settled, and perhaps enjoy a peek at your lovely art collection. Tom's told me all about it."

Tom also declined dessert. No way was he going to let the twins roam unsupervised in a place full of valuable antiques. "If you don't mind, I'll show Lili some of your collection, Dad." When his father waved him away, too, Tom rose and followed Lili out of the room.

After they made sure the twins were glued to the TV in the study, Lili headed toward the four framed landscapes mounted on the entry wall.

"These are yours," she commented.

"How did you guess?"

"I have suspected for a long time that you have an artist's soul," she replied as she peered at the corners of the paintings. "These are unsigned, but I have always sensed there is an artist as well as a businessman inside of you."

What she didn't say was that she and Tom were more alike than he wanted to admit.

Tom gazed after Lili when she turned back to offer to help Megan with the dishes. His mother had hung the paintings long ago. As for his father, Tom doubted that he even gave the artwork more than a passing glance.

Tom began to sense a bond between Lili and himself, something beyond a physical attraction. Uneasy, he reminded himself he had to make her promise to allow his father and him to handle the problem of the center. For a disciplined man like himself who thrived on order, Tom realized a relationship with a determined free spirit like Lili had to be a bad idea.

Or was it?

Twenty minutes later, Lili came back from the kitchen. "Children, please turn off the television and come thank Mr. Eldridge for inviting us here tonight. It is time for us to go home."

Puzzled at the abruptness of her announcement, Tom glanced at his watch. "Are you sure?"

"Yes, it has to be now, before the children's good behavior becomes obvious," Lili said in an undertone. "I think I have accomplished what I said I would do for you—your father didn't look impressed with the children's manners at dinner. Now it is your turn to keep your part of the bargain, yes?"

Tom glanced back to see his father standing in the study doorway watching the children, a pensive expression on his face. Maybe it *was* time to take them home.

As they all said their goodbyes, Tom's admiration for Lili grew. She was a proud woman, and he could only imagine what it had cost her to allow the twins to misbehave in order to honor her bargain with him.

Things might have been different if Lili had been a true "Sullivan woman." Instead, Tom had already figured out that she was a woman with an agenda that didn't seem to include him.

Chapter Seven

Tom was pissed as he put down the phone.

He should have known his father wasn't the type to give up easily. If he had been, he wouldn't have insisted Tom escort Lili to the annual party for Riverview's tenants tonight. Homer was as tenacious as Lili, and it was only too clear to Tom that Lili was, heaven help him, still his father's choice for a daughter-in-law.

As far as Tom was concerned, tonight's command performance wasn't a good idea. He would have passed on the party if he could. After all, in agreeing to go with him, Lili had only been trying to keep up her end of their bargain.

It was time to keep his.

Introducing her to the right people was one way to do it. She'd agreed to stop making fliers, but that didn't guarantee she wouldn't wind up going floor-to-floor and door-to-door throughout the building on her own to drum up financial support for her crusade.

He figured escorting Lili to the party was the wiser choice. He could keep an eye on her, and also introduce her to people they might need to approach in their campaign to save the day care.

At Lili's front door, Tom paused to straighten his shoulders and adjust his formfitting tuxedo jacket. Muttering under his breath, he ran his fingers beneath the too-tight collar of his new white dress shirt in order to give himself room to breathe. A last glance at the sharp crease in his tuxedo trousers assured him he was as ready as he was ever going to be. Ignoring the interested gaze of Lili's next-door neighbor, he took a deep breath to quiet his nerves, eyed the wreath on the door and rang the doorbell.

This time it wasn't one of the twins who answered the door. It was his sister, Megan.

Tom smothered a groan. As if he didn't have a big enough problem on his hands tonight, without his pesky little sister added to the mix. "What are you doing here?"

Unabashed, Megan grinned at his frown. "Hello to you, too! You're looking at tonight's baby-sitter."

"No way!" Tom muttered. "Come on, Meg. You're talking to a guy who's known you since you were in diapers. Did Dad put you up to this?"

Megan looked at him with wide eyes. "What are you talking about?"

Tom had always admired Megan's spirited nature, and looked forward to having her drop in to visit between her travels. He also knew her well enough to see through her feigned innocence. "I happen to know you have less experience with kids than I do!"

Undaunted, she shrugged. "Maybe so, big brother, but the difference between us is that I know how to have fun and you don't. By the time you and Lili get back from the party, I'll have the kids eating out of my hand."

Tom blinked. He didn't know how to have fun?

Maybe so, he thought wryly as he turned a small florist's box over and over in his hands. From the time he'd taken on the family-owned magazine, the only real fun he remembered having had been the day he'd published Lucas Sullivan's inflammatory article and all hell broke loose.

He had to be honest with himself, though. Now that his sister had brought up the sensitive subject of his straight-and-narrow existence, he realized it might be time to have fun.

He fixed Megan with a look that should have silenced her. Instead, her smile only grew broader. "So, did Dad put you up to this?" he demanded again.

Megan held the door open and motioned him inside. "To be honest, it *was* Dad's idea, but I'm actually enjoying the experience. Besides, you ought to know that it's easier to go along with Dad than to argue."

"Yeah," Tom agreed. He hadn't won an argument with his father in years and didn't expect to now. "That's the old man, all right. That's why I was talked into becoming the magazine's publisher when Dad decided to retire. By the time he got through 'reasoning' with me, it was either step up to the plate or sell out. Since I knew how much the magazine means to him, I stayed."

"Dad thinks he's good at problem solving," Megan said with a sympathetic grin. "And since it looks as if you and Lili are the problem of the day, I'm off the hook."

Tom grinned back. Megan reminded him of happier days when their mother was alive and they still lived together as a family. Coming home to an empty place was the pits. Still, when he *did* decide it was time to marry, it was going to be a woman of his own choosing, not his father's. "Lucky me," he said. "How did you get Lili to agree to let you baby-sit?"

"It's a woman thing," Megan replied with a toss of her brown curls. "You wouldn't understand."

"Women!" Tom muttered as he tried to loosen his collar one more time. Either the collar was the wrong size or he was reacting like a schoolboy on his first date.

"You'll get through tonight," Megan assured him. "The truth is that even before Dad asked me to help out, I'd already had a premonition I needed to try to get into the twins' good graces before…" Her voice tailed off.

Tom's antenna was signaling wildly. "If you're talking about me and Lili as a romantic duo, forget it!"

Megan rolled her eyes, bent to pick up a discarded toy and tossed it in a toy chest in front of the fireplace. "Men! It's obvious what Dad's aiming for, even to a guy like you."

"What's wrong with a guy like me?" Tom demanded.

Megan's gaze raked over him from his head to his gleaming new shoes before she shrugged. "I guess you'll do. All I meant was that I wanted to become friends with the twins before Lili decides you're her man and sets out to catch you. Although," she added with an impish grin when Tom's eyebrows rose, "there are moments when I'm not too sure why Lili would want to."

Before Tom could answer, he heard the sound of Lili's voice speaking to the twins. A moment later, she drifted into the room.

Tom's memory of Lili in that unforgettable yellow sundress took second place to tonight's vision.

She was dressed in a slinky black cocktail dress that

not only revealed her womanly curves, but slithered against her body as she moved. Tiny sleeves capped her slender white shoulders, and the neckline dipped to barely cover taut creamy breasts. A slit along one side of the skirt gave him a tantalizing glimpse of a shapely leg, and the hem brushed just below her knees.

Her neck and ears were devoid of jewelry, but Lili carried a small satin evening bag in one hand. A slinky black silk shawl hung over her arm.

Tom forced his gaze away from her dress before he began to speculate on what she could possibly be wearing underneath.

He struggled with a growing need to take Lili in his arms, to kiss the corners of her luminous blue eyes and tell her how beautiful she looked.

Behind Lili, he heard Paulette giggle. It was a good thing Megan and the children were there to remind him that he and Lili weren't alone, or he would have thrown his good intentions to the winds, taken her in his arms and shown her just what she was doing to him. And not only because of her appearance. More and more each day, he'd been discovering the real woman under that facade.

Lili was all woman, Tom thought, and, heaven help him, he needed only one look at her to remind him he was all male. He forced away the erotic thoughts. Under the circumstances, a flesh-and-blood man could stand only so much. She was going to have all the men at the party in the palm of her hand, or his name wasn't Tom Eldridge.

Lili might pretend to look puzzled at the way he was gazing at her, but the blush on her face and the dimple that danced across her right cheek gave her away. She was aware of his reaction to her appearance and, true woman that she'd turned out to be, she was obviously pleased.

If only he could be sure that her stunning appearance tonight wasn't part of her agenda to soften him up.

"Don't forget the corsage," Megan stage-whispered behind him.

Tom eyed the tiny sleeves and low-cut neckline of Lili's dress. There was nowhere to pin the orchid corsage without drawing blood.

"Why don't you put the flowers on Mama's dress?" Paulette asked. "That's what they do in the movies."

Put to shame by this precocious six-year-old, Tom figured he had no choice. He took the corsage out of the box and gingerly tried to pin it to the front of Lili's dress. While trying to grasp enough of the dainty material in one hand, he pricked his finger.

"Ouch!" he muttered. To his disgust, blood was welling up on his fingertip.

"Mon Dieu!" Lili grasped his hand. "Paulette, hurry and find Mr. Eldridge a Band-Aid! There's a box on the shelf in the bathroom."

"I know where it is!" Paulette ran out of the room. "I'll be right back."

Tom tried to draw his hand away. Lili's touch was more than he'd bargained for. "I'm fine, really."

Lili ignored his protest and reached for the bandage Paulette was waving in the air. Obviously a pro at such matters, she applied it to Tom's finger. "There," she said happily. "You'll feel better soon."

Tom closed his eyes. Feeling better was a matter of opinion. What he did know was that there was nothing like a Bugs Bunny Band-Aid to cool a man's libido.

THE RIVERVIEW'S PENTHOUSE had been cleared and turned into a ballroom. Small tables ringed the room, and crystal chandeliers illuminated the couples slowly revolving in time to soft music.

Tom drew the black satin wrap off Lili's shoulders and handed it to a waiting attendant. By the time he'd turned back to her, she was standing at the French doors that led to the ballroom. True to his predictions, she was already drawing a great deal of attention from the men.

Tom glanced around the room and noticed a few women enviously eyeing Lili. Not that he could blame them. Whether she'd intended it or not, Lili was a blazing figure of sensuality tonight.

His fixed smile faded when he recognized the open lust on more than one man's face. He had to fight the temptation to take her by the arm and hide her in a corner before all hell broke loose.

Then he remembered that part of the bargain he'd made with Lili was to introduce her to the movers and shakers in the room.

He owed her that much. At least he'd be there to keep an eye on the situation.

He touched her on the shoulder. "Care to dance?"

Lili nodded. The captivated look in Tom's eyes made the cocktail dress she'd splurged on worth every penny. Maybe she'd managed to cross an invisible line without realizing it, but her plan was working. And all because she'd wanted Tom to notice her as a woman, not just part of a bargain they'd made. Not only to notice her, she thought with a shiver of anticipation, but to have him want her as a woman, just as she wanted him as a man.

She'd forgotten that the dress might be considered a

blatant sexual invitation by anyone who didn't understand a woman's right to feel good about herself.

Grateful that Tom's body would shield her from disapproving eyes, Lili melted into his waiting arms and leaned her head against his shoulder.

The arms that held her so tightly were strong and sure. She breathed in his scent, a mixture of spice and a faint hint of musk—a scent that reminded her of all she'd once had and lost, and yearned to have again.

The other couples on the dance floor faded from Lili's thoughts. The romantic song playing in the background—"All I Want Is You," from *The Phantom of the Opera*—was surely meant to be a message. Tonight, all she wanted was Tom.

Tom *must* feel the same way, Lili thought when his warm breath teased the side of her throat before it moved up to her lips.

She looked up at him, only to meet his rueful smile and raised eyebrow. He was right. While he might share her feelings tonight, they were in full sight of the people she needed to approach for help. She straightened proudly and smiled back.

"Are you okay?" Tom asked softly as he twirled her around the dance floor.

Lili wasn't sure what Tom meant by "okay," but here in his arms tonight, she felt more complete as a woman than she had in the last four years.

Nodding, she lost herself in his strong yet tender embrace. His solid chest, the slight pressure of his hand against her back as he guided her around the floor, made her feel womanly and maybe, she thought dimly, even cherished.

"Very okay," she finally murmured as she moved to the music, following Tom as effortlessly as if they'd been dancing together for years instead of for the first time. "I could dance like this all night."

"Me, too," he said, his lips touching hers in a brief, warm caress.

She smiled and slid her fingers through the soft brown hair that curled at the nape of his neck. At his murmur of pleasure, she slipped them under his collar and caressed his warm skin. His heartbeat was strong against her cheek, his voice soft and low as he laughingly acknowledged her caress and murmured in her ear.

She was too caught up in heightened sensations to hear what Tom was saying, but it didn't matter. For now, it would have to be enough to be held in his arms the way she'd often dreamed he would hold her. Enough to inhale the male scent of him, to know that for these few moments tonight he belonged to her and only her.

"What would you like to do next?" Tom asked when the music stopped and the dancers applauded and broke into small groups. "I'm sure you must have a plan," he added with a wry smile.

Shaken out of her sensuous reverie, Lili glanced around the dance floor. Under Tom's interested gaze, she tugged at the neckline of her dress. "Finding somewhere private for a moment would be a good idea."

Tom checked out the room. The small tables scattered around the dance floor were all taken. People were crowded three deep at the bars set in all four corners. To make matters worse, by remaining in the center of the ballroom, they were drawing attention. "How about the balcony?"

"Yes, but a cool drink would be nice." Lili fanned herself with the back of her hand. "It is very warm in here, no?"

"Yes," he agreed, with a smile at Lili's unique way of tuning no into a question. "A glass of champagne?"

Before Lili could answer, he took two champagne flutes from the tray of a passing waiter, and glanced over her shoulder. "How about taking our drinks outside?"

Lili felt a delicious shiver run through her as she followed Tom out to a long balcony. Diamondlike stars were strewn across a deep blue velvet sky, and one seemed to hang suspended, blinking, from a luminous new moon. The muted sounds of city traffic twenty stories below dueled with the soft spring breeze, and the scent of decorative greenery teased her senses.

An amorous couple kissing in a secluded corner drew Lili's attention. If only that could have been her and Tom, she thought.

"Lili?" His low baritone broke into her reverie. He was holding out a glass of champagne. "Do you still want that cool drink?"

Lili glanced away from the lovers and into Tom's warm brown eyes. Eyes that seemed to soften as they gazed at her. She took the offered glass. "I am sorry. I am afraid the beauty of the evening stole my thoughts away."

Tom understood all too well how Lili felt. He, too, had been lost in admiration of the brilliant moon. Only his admiration had been for the moon's reflection in Lili's eyes and in the wistful smile on her face. If he didn't do something to get his mind off places he'd already decided he had no business visiting, he was a goner for sure. "Mind telling me what you were thinking?"

Lili shook her head. How could she tell Tom she'd been wondering how it would feel to have his lips press against hers again, this time lingering long enough to satisfy her hunger? Or of having his searching tongue caressing hers the same way his eyes caressed her bare shoulders?

How could she tell Tom that for the first time in four years her body trembled at a man's touch?

How could she tell him that tonight she desired him in all the ways a woman could desire a man? A man she'd fallen in love with but who didn't love her back.

If only she was able to blame her sensuous thoughts on the lovely night that surrounded them—thoughts that surely would fade when she was back in familiar surroundings.

If only her heart wasn't keeping time with the strains of a lilting waltz coming through the open doors behind her, she might be able to keep her end of the bargain they'd agreed to.

If only they were lovers in truth instead of reluctant partners in a masquerade.

"It *is* beautiful out here tonight," she finally murmured.

Tom was caught by the dreamy look on Lili's face. He knew, given a little encouragement, he would take advantage of the moment and show her just what *he* was thinking.

Suddenly, the photograph of Lili's late husband flashed through his mind, and those warning eyes. That look that said he was being trusted to do the right thing.

"I think I'll go and find something to eat with the champagne," he said, without waiting for Lili to answer. "I'll be right back."

Lili hid a rueful smile as Tom turned on his heel and disappeared into the ballroom. He seemed as frustrated as she was.

She walked over to the door and watched him cross the room to buffet tables covered with plates of fancy appetizers. He was easily one of the more attractive men in the room, and she could hardly wait to see if he would take her in his arms again.

Tom was quite different from her beloved late husband. Paul had been blond, tall and slender, with dancing hazel eyes and a sense of humor that had always left her laughing.

Tom, on the other hand, was a man of average build, broad shoulders, dark brown hair and sensuous brown eyes that had spoken to her from the first day they'd met. The strange part of it all, she thought with a smile, was that she was the only woman in her group of friends who thought Tom was sexy.

She glanced over the parapet while she waited for him to come back. Off to one side, twenty floors below, passing automobile lights resembled fireflies, and beneath her, the Chicago River flowed between concrete banks lined with colorful lights.

Behind her, the party and the chance to meet possible donors called to her. She took a deep breath. She had to stop dreaming about Tom and try to remember she was here tonight merely as his date, nothing more. Sooner or later his father would have to get the message that Tom wasn't interested in marriage, and their charade would be over.

By the time he came back, balancing two plates of goodies, Lili was surrounded by a group of plainly lustful men. He felt a pang of jealousy as he realized he shouldn't have been surprised to find the male guests had discovered her. They were obviously wondering who she was and trying to wangle an introduction. He wondered if Lili reciprocated their interest.

Tom froze at the thought. For all intents and purposes Lili was his date for the duration of their bargain. He had her verbal agreement on that and he wasn't going to let her forget it.

The trouble was that he knew some of the men. Rick Hayes, the owner of a series of successful travel agencies, was in the process of ending his third marriage. Renaldo Perez, a suave and sophisticated jeweler, was said to be toying with the idea of marriage to a second wife. Pete Borden, normally a decent enough man, was single and the CEO of an advertising agency. Unfortunately, he was known to have a track record of broken engagements.

The biggest problem of all was that Lili was naive when it came to dealing with men. Otherwise she would never have made a bargain with Tom himself.

He'd promised to find a fairy godfather to take on Lili's cause, but it was obvious he was going to have to prevent her from giving away her identity as the brains behind the troubling petitions and fliers. The men might be less likely to help out if that happened. He wanted to approach them first.

Out of the corner of her eye, Lili saw Tom striding toward her. The grim look on his face gave him away; he was jealous. She was pleased.

"Oh good, you're back," she said, drawing him to her side. "Come and meet my new acquaintances."

Tom eyed the men politely, but he was seething inside. Since all three of these guys had a reputation for hitting on women, he intended to set them straight before things went too far. "We've already met."

"How come you've been keeping this lovely lady for yourself, Tom?" Renaldo asked with a lewd glance at Lili.

"Yeah," Rick echoed. "Hardly fair for the rest of us."

Pete Borden's eyes were mentally undressing Lili.

Tom had had enough. Sexual teasing wasn't exactly new, but these three looked as if they meant it.

Tom thrust a plate of food at Lili. "Take off, fellows," he said. "The lady is busy."

The men protested, but Tom had a good idea how to cool them down. "How's the wife doing since her accident, Renaldo?" he said with a glance over his shoulder at the dance floor. "I take it she isn't here tonight?"

Renaldo flushed. "No, Ellie said she had a headache and preferred to stay home and rest."

Tom nodded. He knew damn well Ellie Perez's headache was her philandering husband. "Rick, heard you just racked up your third divorce and got hit with a million dollar alimony suit."

Rick Hayes merely shrugged. "Win some, lose some. It's only money."

"Then I guess you'll be generous when Lili and I ask you for a sizable donation to her latest cause—keeping Riverview's child care center open." Tom turned to the man beside him. "You, too, Renaldo?"

Perez reluctantly nodded.

"That would be wonderful," Lili said with a brilliant smile that eased the tension. "I can't thank you men enough."

"You too, Pete?"

"Yeah, I guess," Pete answered with an envious glance at Tom. "See you around."

After telling Lili what a pleasure it had been to meet her, the three men headed back to the ballroom.

So much for worrying about Lili, Tom thought. Given the chance, she'd have everyone eating out of her hands before the night was over.

He waited until the men were out of sight. "So, now that you've found three godfathers, where do we go from here?"

Lili was secretly delighted at the jaundiced look on Tom's face. He *was* jealous. "You didn't have to worry about me," she said with a sweet smile. "I am a grown woman and I have been married before. I know enough about men to know these didn't mean any harm. Besides, it is normal for a man to admire a woman, or for a woman to admire a man she is interested in, no?"

Given a perfect opening, Tom decided to take the plunge. It was now or never—the chance to ask the question that had been bothering him for days. "And how do you feel about me?"

Lili smiled over the rim of her glass. "As I have said, I am a woman and you are an attractive man."

Tom was pleased. "You're definitely a woman, Lili," he said sincerely as he took her measure. "That's part of the problem."

Lili might be teasing him, Tom thought, but he had nothing to lose by taking up the challenge he saw in her eyes. "Instead of spending the rest of the night sticking around here, I think this might be a good time for us to talk things over, don't you? In fact, I'm sure of it," he hurriedly added before Lili could answer. "We have to come up with some rules or even guidelines in this crazy relationship of ours."

Lili motioned to the other couples on the balcony. "Perhaps a more private place?"

Tom sensed from the warm look in her eyes that they were no longer just talking about trying to keep a mutually convenient bargain. As for him, he had finally realized he didn't want a typical "Sullivan woman." What he wanted was Lili, no matter who she turned out to be.

Bargain be damned.

They had to talk. Now. Tonight.

He heard himself asking, "Your place or mine?" When Lili's eyes lit up, he hurried to add, "I guess I shouldn't have put it like that. I should have said how about your place? The twins are bound to be asleep by now."

Lili's eyebrows rose. "I am sure Megan won't mind watching the children a little longer. How about your place?"

Tom swallowed hard. To hell with talking about bargains or agreements. This might be the chance to show Lili how much he cared for her. "You're sure?"

She smiled. "I am very sure."

Chapter Eight

Lili felt Tom's warmth as he drove them to his place. Overhead the sky had grown cloudy and the moon was nowhere in sight. A jagged flash of lightning tore through the sky. Lili shivered.

Seconds later, a distant clap of thunder sounded. A thrill shot through her that had nothing to do with the approaching storm outside. Inside her, another storm was moving in fast, setting every fiber of her body tingling with anticipation.

Tom's place turned out to be a loft on the third floor of a renovated factory building. She'd expected him to live in a luxurious condo in the same part of the city as his father, but she wasn't really surprised. She'd long suspected Tom wasn't the man he appeared to be around the magazine.

It started to pour just as he came around the car and opened the door for her. He glanced at her bare legs and high-heeled sandals. With a wry shrug, he took off his jacket and held it over her head. "Let's get you inside before you get drenched."

"How about you?" Lili protested as the rain quickly soaked Tom's shirt, revealing a muscular chest covered with dark brown curls. Before she realized what he intended to do, he picked her up in his arms and, shielding her from the rain, strode toward the rain to the entrance of the building.

All too aware of Tom's innate sensuality, Lili let him press her against his shoulder. This was what she'd longed for and had almost given up finding, she thought as she snuggled against the solid warmth of him.

Her stomach tensed when she saw the elevator. An old freight lift with waist-high walls, it was surely a relic from the time when the building was used as a factory.

"You can put me down now."

"No way," he said with a wicked smile that made her body warm and her heart skip. "Not when I've finally got you where I want you."

Laughing at Tom's unexpected show of humor, she shook drops of water from her hair. "We are just in time to avoid the main part of the storm, no?"

"We are just in time, yes." Smiling into Lili's eyes, Tom bent over her and kissed the drops away.

How could he not have noticed the finely etched laugh lines at the edges of her deep sapphire eyes? he wondered as he unlocked the door to his place and carried her inside. How could he resist stroking the silky blond hair that flowed around her piquant face?

He figured he must have been blind not to have responded to Lili's exquisite personality before tonight. How could he have not taken the time to really look at this delightful, lovely woman?

He stood her on her feet and gestured around him. "Nothing fancy, but I call this home."

Lili gazed around the converted factory loft. The interior walls were a soothing mossy green, the woodwork a soft taupe. A beige couch covered with dark green cushions sat before a fireplace, and on the polished hardwood floor in front of the couch was a small forest-green throw rug.

Tom was definitely not a nester, she thought as she gazed at an area against the wall that served as a small functional kitchen. Two stools stood in front of a counter that separated the kitchen area from the rest of the loft. Off to one side, a brick partition separated what appeared to be a bedroom from the rest of the living space.

Lightning flashed, and she was drawn to the floor-to-ceiling windows at the far end of the room. Here the area had been converted into a studio. A drafting table was splattered with paint, and over it were scattered an artist's tools: a well-used palette, pastels, tubes of fresh oils, brushes, pencils and bits of charcoal.

Lili's heart warmed as her suspicions about Tom were confirmed. He *was* actually two men. One, a no-nonsense, pragmatic magazine publisher. The other an artist.

"Lovely," she murmured as she wandered over to admire a series of landscape paintings mounted on the walls, showing gradual changes of the seasons. From the modest initials in the righthand corner of each one, it was evident these were more of Tom's work. Then she noticed the unfinished sketch of a woman that was propped on an easel.

"If you did this, you have the soul of a true artist," Lili murmured as she studied the sketch. "It cannot be easy for you to have taken over the magazine from your father when you have such an obvious talent as this."

Tom shrugged. "We don't always have the luxury of

choice. I took over the magazine for my father's sake. I paint in my free time."

As a single mother of two children, Lili understood not always having the luxury of choice. Her heart went out to Tom.

"Who is the woman?"

"Someone I met recently," Tom said as he drew Lili's damp shawl off her shoulders with a murmur of appreciation. The look in his eyes told her that while she might have had to settle for a fleeting kiss earlier, tonight she wouldn't have anything less than the real man.

Tom turned away to hang up his wet jacket. How could he tell Lili that the woman in the sketch was meant to be her? That he'd started it as soon as he'd come home from the company picnic? Or that the reason the drawing, intended to be an oil painting of Lili, remained unfinished was that he'd realized he didn't know the real woman?

Before the night was over, he hoped that would change. Only when he found the real Lili would he be able to complete the portrait.

Lili went back to studying the sketch. "I can read the seductive look in the woman's eyes," she said softly. "She looks as if she is inviting you into an embrace."

"I wish," Tom murmured, his voice barely audible.

Lili sensed a growing sexual tension between them and she glanced over at Tom. A yearning look had come into his eyes. She'd been right. Something had definitely changed between them.

The storm outside was growing stronger now. Lili turned to look out the studio windows. Dark clouds drifted by the windows, accompanied by heavy rain. "There is no point in even thinking of your taking me home soon, is there?"

"Not if I can help it," Tom answered fervently.

Lili smiled at the urgency she heard in his voice, and gestured to the unfinished sketch. "If the model is truly like this, then she must be a passionate woman." As she lowered her arm, one tiny sleeve fell off her shoulder. She sighed and tugged it back into place. "You wished to talk?"

"Yes, but not about art or the portrait." Tom turned away from the unexpected glimpse of her lush breasts, but not before he noticed a conspiratorial smile on Lili's face.

"Art is a language we both understand, no?" she said.

Tom's body stirred in response to that smile. It was time to take the plunge. "Perhaps, but I believe I know another language we might both understand."

He'd initially intended to talk about renegotiating their agreement, he thought righteously. To tell Lili he was no longer able to think of her only as a partner in a convenient relationship. He wanted to tell her that to-night he had seen her as if for the first time. And to tell her how much he was attracted to her. If he didn't put his cards on the table soon, he was afraid he wouldn't be able to play them at all. The only problem left was that their relationship was changing so fast, he wasn't sure if he was making a fool of himself.

Still…

The expression on Lili's face seemed to say she was a woman proud of her own sensuality. That she was aware of and shared this feeling of sexual tension be-tween them. Without stopping to think, Tom gave in to the impulse he'd been fighting all night. He pulled Lili to him, raised her chin and kissed her, gently at first, then with all the pent-up desire in him.

"Mon Dieu," he heard her whisper. Her sultry smile as she gazed at him was the smile he'd tried to capture when he'd started to sketch her from memory. It was frankly challenging, perhaps even daring him to return her unspoken invitation. "I am ready for you to speak in any language you choose," she invited him with an impish grin.

Tom was unprepared for the invitation. "In a minute," he replied, stalling for time to make sure he'd read her right. No matter how eager he was, the last thing he wanted was to end a promising relationship before it started.

"Hungry?" he asked. "You didn't eat much at the party. How about raiding the refrigerator while we talk?"

Lili seemed amused by his question. "If that is what you truly wish. Perhaps a bit of cheese and a glass of wine?"

At the teasing glint in her eyes, Tom smothered a groan at his foolishness. What he should be doing was taking off that sexy dress and making love to every inch of her fascinating body. Not standing here talking nonsense. They should be in bed, where he could show her what he truly wanted, even though the last thing he needed was someone turning his life upside down.

On the other hand, even his friend Lucas had confessed that, given the right reasons, the six rules on the mating game could be bent, broken or even ignored. *Good enough,* Tom thought rapidly. Considering how he felt about Lili, he was in the mood to ignore all of Sullivan's Rules.

He took a bottle of zinfandel from the refrigerator, fixed some sharp cheese on a plate and plunked some washed grapes in a bowl. Once he'd poured them each a glass of wine, he said, "Maybe we'd better talk about this relationship of ours before things go too far."

"Yes, if you think so," Lili agreed. Smiling seductively over the rim of her glass, she slowly sipped the cool, honey-colored wine. "You may go first."

The laughter in Lili's eyes was enough to send Tom's testosterone through the roof. To hell with talking, he told himself. He was through waiting for the right moment; this had to be it. He intended to show Lili how much he wanted her.

Frustrated, he ran his fingers through his hair. "Lili," he warned, "I originally intended to spend the evening renegotiating our bargain, but I have to tell you you're not making it easy for me. That look in your eyes is turning my mind into mush."

Lili set her glass of wine on the table. No innocent, she knew what men thought of women who teased. She didn't want Tom to think of her as one of them.

"To feel desire is no shame," she said softly as she moved closer to him and undid the top button of his damp shirt. "The truth is it has been too long since I first wished for you to hold me." She undid another button, then another. "No more talking. What I wish is for you to make love to me now."

Tom forgot any lingering reservations he might have had. He placed his hands on either side of Lili's head and tilted it upward. "You're sure about this? Once we start, I don't intend to turn back."

"I am very sure," Lili whispered as she found herself in Tom's close embrace. "And you?"

In answer, he brushed his lips across hers and tasted, then tasted again. "Me, too."

With a low murmur of pleasure, Lili lost herself in the sound of Tom's smoldering voice, the fresh scent of rain in his damp hair and the promise in his eyes.

His warm, naked chest and the strong beat of his heart against her cheek were more intoxicating than champagne or wine. As she gave in to the fiery sensations running through her, she knew that if heaven was a place where dreams came true, then it must be right here in Tom's arms tonight.

"I want you," she breathed when Tom finally released her. "And you? Do you want me for the woman I am or the woman you want me to be?"

"I want—" he began, before a flash of lightning and a clap of thunder drowned out the rest of his reply. Thunder had always frightened Lili, and she nestled further into his embrace. Her emotions were so tangled she could hardly think. An intense longing shot through her, and when Tom murmured reassuringly and held her closer still, she gave up thinking.

Whatever he wanted to talk about no longer mattered. She had married her husband for love and given birth to their two beautiful children. Her husband would always be part of her life, but she was long past mourning. Tonight she wanted to feel like a woman—a woman who was falling in love with a man.

Tonight, every nerve in her body told her that making love with Tom would be a new experience. Tonight was a time for dreams, and Tom would be the one to fulfill them. Tonight, she would be all woman for her man.

"Love me well," she murmured, holding out her hands to him.

"I will—I promise," Tom said, as he lost himself in the miracle of Lili's embrace.

The sounds of the gathering storm outside seemed to fade, but the thunder pounding in Tom's heart grew heavier. He began to feel that the gods who watched over foolish men like him were smiling down on him tonight. He wanted Lili in a way he'd never wanted a woman before, and, thank heaven, it was obvious she wanted him, too.

He lifted her into his arms and strode to the alcove that was his bedroom. Growing desire raced through him when, murmuring in pleasure, she leaned out of his embrace to throw the bedspread aside.

Tom lowered her to the bed. The pristine sheets beneath her exquisite body became an artist's canvas, with the lovely Lili the subject. No wonder he hadn't been able to complete the sketch, he thought as he gazed down at the appealing picture she made, her inviting smile touching him in ways he hadn't known he could be touched.

Lili seemed to change moment by fascinating moment. How could he have hoped to capture that elusive quality on canvas? Tonight, she'd changed from an ethereal woman into an enchanting siren able to capture his senses with a simple glance.

He smiled down at Lili and ran his hand lightly along the hem of her slinky black cocktail dress. "Need some help with this?"

Lost in a haze of desire, Lili glanced down at herself. The sleeves of the dress had fallen off her shoulders, revealing her black lace bra. The rest of the dress was bunched up around her waist, showing her thighs and a glimpse of black lace panties. She was capable of rising and undressing herself, but the invitation in Tom's voice was too heated to ignore. "The sooner the better, as you say in this country. No?"

"The sooner the better, yes." Tom grinned and set to work. He lifted Lili in his arms and slid her dress off in one swift movement, then eased her back onto the bed, admiring the dramatic effect of her black underwear against the white sheets. Reaching behind her, he unfastened her lacy bra and tugged it down her arms. Without panty hose, it was a simple matter to hook his thumbs in her black thong and pull it down over her hips and her legs.

"Now you." Lili slid across the bed to make room for Tom. "Do you need any help?" she teased, even as she undid the last button on his shirt.

Tom managed to hide a grin at her question. If he let her undress him, their mutual seduction would be over before it began. "Better not," he chuckled, and drew away. "Not if I want this moment to last, and I do."

He shucked the rest of his damp clothing and dropped down on the bed beside Lili. Before he gathered her into his arms, he reached inside the nightstand drawer and drew out protection.

In moments, they were skin to skin, heartbeat to heartbeat, lips to lips. Lili slid down Tom's chest and kissed his hard nipples.

The sensation of her warm tongue almost made him lose control. Muttering under his breath, he flipped Lili over, cupped her breasts in his hands and bent to tongue and kiss each golden aureole. "This has to be a dream," he said.

"Then I am glad we are having the same dream," Lili sighed as she arched into his embrace. "More, please."

He stilled her with a gentle finger on her lips. "This is no dream," he said as he fitted himself between her legs. "Give me a moment and I'll prove it to you."

'Oh my!" She gasped in pleasure when Tom parted her thighs and caressed the delicate folds of skin.

"This is only the beginning," he assured her.

Lili shivered as Tom kissed his way down her waist to her legs and proceeded to pay close attention to each of her toes. When he moved back to the inside of her thighs, she grasped his hair and pulled him up to her. "No more," she protested, holding out her arms to him. "I want to feel you inside me."

"My pleasure." Tom nudged her knees apart, then slid his hands to her waist. Holding her in place, he entered her with a single thrust.

Lili felt as if she were floating in some mystical world where the moon and stars were smiling down on her. It was like a fantasy come true, she thought dimly as a shower of shooting stars fell around her.

Tom's pace quickened, and she lifted her hips in a matching rhythm. Seconds later, he groaned, and with a deep, final thrust, sent her spinning through space.

They collapsed in each other's arms, and Lili cuddled into Tom's heated chest. She had almost fallen asleep when she felt him stir and get out of bed.

"Lili? Are you awake?"

She opened her eyes to see him handing her a terry-cloth robe. "Come with me?"

Wrapped in the robe, she took his hand and followed him to a bench in the corner of the studio. Sleepily, she yawned and hung back. "Where are we going?"

"You'll see." He drew the robe down over her shoulders. "Sit here and don't move until I tell you to, please." He adjusted the robe around her, leaving one shoulder bare, with a tantalizing glimpse of breast. Ignoring her blush, he moved to the easel and set up a fresh canvas.

After a moment's thoughtful hesitation, he picked up a pastel crayon and began to draw.

"The model is intended to be me?" Lili asked, fascinated by the intent look on Tom's face. "And why tonight?" When he didn't reply, she asked again. "Tom?"

"I want to capture the special aura you have about you tonight," he said absently. "No," he ordered when she started to protest. "Please, don't move."

"What is this 'aura'?" Mesmerized by the look in Tom's eyes, Lili glanced down at herself. In bed, making love, nudity had its place, but having her bare form on canvas was somehow different. For the first time, she felt embarrassed at the way Tom gazed at her.

Tom drew swiftly, shading in Lili's eyes with sapphire pastels. He wanted to capture both her vitality and sexuality. "You'll see in a moment. At least I hope so."

There was more to Lili than her sexuality, Tom realized as he chose a pastel pink to shade her cheeks. She was intelligent, warm, and when making love, brimming with life. Even so, he realized that until he knew her well enough, he'd never be able to do justice to her in a painting.

After half an hour had passed, Lili felt she couldn't sit quietly for another moment. "May I move now?"

Tom sighed, put down the pastel he'd been using and motioned Lili to his side. "What do you think?"

She gazed at the canvas. The subject's sapphire eyes were wide and luminous. The long blond hair was tousled, as if she'd just arisen from bed after making love. Which, Lili thought with a guilty blush, was the truth. In the portrait, her lips were parted in a Mona Lisa smile, and she had the look of a woman who had been thoroughly and exquisitely loved.

"Are you sure that is me?" she whispered, unable to believe she actually looked this way.

Tom ran his hand over her shoulder and she shivered. "You're cold. I'm sorry," he said as he turned her to face him. "Forgive me?"

In answer, she slipped her arms around him.

Tom eyed the sketch critically. "It's pretty close, but I'm not sure I'm there yet." He picked her up and carried her back to the bedroom. "I'm afraid we'll just have to practice until I get it right."

A willing student, Lili could hardly wait while Tom drew off her robe, kissed her senseless, then fell onto the bed with her once more.

"Practice makes perfect," she heard him murmur as he molded his body to hers and with a swift thrust took her back into the starlit heavens with him.

An hour later, she awakened to find Tom leaning over her and gently caressing her breasts with a forefinger. Blushing at his warm and knowing look, she drew the blanket up to her chin. "What time is it?"

"Almost midnight." Smiling, he gently pulled the cover back down to her waist. "You're much too lovely to hide," he said as he bent to tongue the sensitive spot beneath her chin.

Lili gasped and tried to sit up. "Midnight! What will your sister think of me?"

Tom drew her back into his arms, laving her heated skin with his tongue. "If I know Megan, she'll probably think we're having too good a time to come home until the party's finally over. Don't worry, Cinderella," he added with a wicked grin, "if I don't get you back before midnight, my car won't turn into a pumpkin."

Lili felt her body come alive yet again under Tom's

erotic attention. "My goodness!" she gasped. "I have never done anything like this before!"

"Then it's time you did," he said, kissing his way down to her breasts. "But only with me. Tonight is meant to be just for the two of us." He teased first one nipple, then the other, with his tongue, bringing them each to a hard peak.

Inhaling shakily, Lili held him to her and smiled tenderly. Tom had taken her to heights she had never known before, and in the process, she sensed a bond had been forged. Never again would she feel alone.

"Do you want to go home?" Tom asked her, running a finger along the inside of her thigh.

"No." Lili's nerve ends quivered at his touch. "I have not changed my mind about staying with you tonight, but I would feel better if you called your sister and told her we will be delayed. She will worry about us."

Tom considered the tiny mole on her stomach with interest. "How about I tell Megan you've decided on a sleepover?"

Lili frowned. "What is this 'sleepover'?"

"It's what we call spending the night at a friend's house. After tonight, I'd say we're definitely friends, wouldn't you?" He gave her a wicked grin. "Knowing Megan, I'm sure she'll be happy to cooperate."

When Lili nodded, Tom picked up the phone on the nightstand, dialed her home number and spoke rapidly into the phone. "Yeah," he admitted after listening for a moment, "but I'd like to keep this between us. Okay? Thanks, Meg, I owe you one."

Lili flinched when a clap of thunder shook the building and rattled the loft's windows.

"Don't be afraid," Tom murmured into her ear. "I'll keep you safe."

"Still, maybe we should get back before the storm wakes up the twins."

"Not to worry," he answered with another kiss. "Megan will call if they need you. She's curious as a cat and will have a lot of questions. You don't have to answer them if you don't want to. Anyway, I'm sure she'll be as happy to stay at your place as I am to have you here."

Lili paused to listen for a moment. "It is still raining outside?"

"Buckets," Tom declared, his mind more on Lili than the storm. "Why?"

"Then there is no point in even thinking of getting wet again," she said wickedly. "Come back to me, my Tom. We will love again and see the morning in together."

TRUE TO HIS WORD, Tom took Lili home just as dawn broke over Lake Michigan. He would have carried her up the steps and kissed her long and deep if they hadn't been in plain sight.

"Sleep well," he whispered as she unlocked the front door and started into the house.

"Thanks to you, *chèri,* I am sure I will." She smiled happily, then blew him a last kiss before she closed the door.

Tom stood on the porch a moment. There would never be enough time for loving Lili, he thought wryly. Too bad they still had to come to some kind of an agreement over this surprising new turn in their relationship.

He finally shrugged and headed for his car with

mixed feelings. He knew that his life had undergone a change, yet he was also aware that not everything had altered. Lili was still a woman who, according to their bargain, was to go on masquerading as his fiancée. And unless he was mistaken, she was determined to go on with her crusade.

The problem was that Lili had touched him in a thousand ways, and he wanted what had happened between them to be their own private heaven.

Chapter Nine

Monday morning's mail brought Tom the summons to a special meeting of Riverview's business tenants. A handwritten note at the bottom of his invitation asked him to drop by the management's office prior to the meeting. To add to his growing unease about the outcome of the command performance, the terse note was signed by Jules Kagan, Riverview's owner.

Not a good sign.

If he'd read the invitation right, and Tom was afraid he had, there was trouble looming on the horizon. Unless he could persuade Lili to quit antagonizing Riverview's management, Judgment Day was two weeks away.

After the wonderful night he'd spent with Lili, the last thing he wanted was to be reminded of the building management's jaundiced view of her activities. With a muttered curse, he crushed the summons and tossed it into the wastebasket, where, in his opinion, it belonged.

Kagan didn't know of Lili's unapologetic determination to keep the center open, or he wouldn't have postponed the day of reckoning. He would have taken her on now, Tom mused angrily. Recalling the stubborn look in Lili's eyes whenever he suggested she give up and let him take over her crusade, he figured his chances of changing her mind were nil.

Furthermore, he strongly suspected Lili believed that only a coward would give in without a fight.

He couldn't blame her for that. He felt the same way.

He had no one but himself to blame for the stalemate, he told himself as he paced the office floor. To make matters worse, it was too late for second thoughts about the wisdom of keeping Lili in his life. It seemed that he'd already fallen in love with her.

Muttering under his breath, he fished the crumpled memo out of the basket, smoothed it and read it again before he cursed and put it in his pocket. Throwing away bad news didn't make it go away. Somehow, he had to show Lili that Kagan meant business, before it was too late.

Actually, the problem was a no-brainer, he thought wryly as he strode out of the office to take the elevators to the art studio on the floor below. Lili was guilty of stirring up the employees and he had to get her to quit. He should ignore the surprising depth of his feelings for her and do what he had to do with any employee who acted against management's policy.

Lili was an intelligent woman, he told himself as he approached the studio. Surely she would understand his position. Ergo, all he had to do was show her the memo and ask her to back off while there was still time. If she resisted, he'd threaten to fire her. He wouldn't think about how much having Lili close by and working in the magazine's art studio had brightened his days.

Tom found her pinning fresh paper on her drawing

board. The large picture windows on three sides of the studio bathed her in sunlight and turned her hair to gold.

He paused to admire the compelling picture she made, and had to put his hands in his pockets to keep from reaching for her. Since they were alone, he wanted to pull her into his arms and capture that elusive smile with his lips.

He couldn't, not without tempting fate. Not since he'd discovered that Lili was able to make love with just a look. He felt in his pocket for the "invitation." Thank goodness he'd remembered to bring it with him or she'd never believe it when he told her he had to put the magazine ahead of their unusual relationship for now.

It was imperative to impress on her that not only the future of the magazine might be at stake, but the jobs of several hundred of the building's employees if she continued to antagonize Kagan.

Lili greeted him with a bright smile and that adorable tilt of her head, reminding him of the way he'd tried to capture her on canvas. Heaven help him, he thought as his resolution to be firm with her grew shaky.

"Good morning, Tom." Her warm look suggested she wanted to be kissed, and Tom discovered that even the subtle invitation could be as sexually exciting as the kiss itself.

Remembering why he was here, he took a deep breath.

"Good morning, Lili," he said casually. "As long as we're both early this morning, I figured this is a good time for that talk I spoke about."

Lili's lovely smile faded. "Of course."

Tom felt like all kinds of a jerk, but he didn't see that he had a choice here.

"I wanted to thank you for Saturday night."

"You wish to *thank* me for Saturday night?"

Now there was a hurt look in her eyes at his unfeeling remark. Surely, after their amazing night together, she had to be bewildered at the change in him.

"I'm sorry, Lili. Let me back up a minute. I'm afraid that didn't come out the way I meant it to. Actually, I just wanted to thank you for having kept our bargain and coming to the tenants' party. I'm not saying it very well, but what I want to tell you is that as far as I'm concerned, after Saturday night, your end of the bargain is over."

Her eyes narrowed. "*My* part of the bargain is over?" she asked in a thin voice that made Tom's blood run cold.

He damned himself a hundred times at the change that came over Lili. Gone was the warm look in her eyes and the suggestion of a kiss on her smiling lips. He should have told her he was only trying to get her to back off and let him take care of her crusade. And, unfortunately for him, the only way he'd figured he could make that happen was to cool their relationship for a while.

From the way Lili was staring at him, it looked as if he was damned if he tried to protect her and damned if he didn't. He had to remind himself he was here largely to save Lili from herself.

He reached into his pocket, took out the summons to the meeting and silently held it out to her. After reading it, she looked up at him. "What does this have to do with me?"

"I'm afraid it has everything to do with you, Lili," he said. "It's about those fliers you're still making, even

GET FREE BOOKS and a FREE GIFT WHEN YOU PLAY THE...

SLOT MACHINE GAME!

Just scratch off the silver box with a coin. Then check below to see the gifts you get!

YES! I have scratched off the silver box. Please send me the 2 free Harlequin American Romance® books and gift for which I qualify. I understand I am under no obligation to purchase any books, as explained on the back of this card.

354 HDL D7WZ   154 HDL D7XF

FIRST NAME

LAST NAME

ADDRESS

APT.#   CITY

STATE/PROV.   ZIP/POSTAL CODE

7	7	7	**Worth TWO FREE BOOKS** plus a **BONUS** Mystery Gift!
🍒	🍒	🍒	**Worth TWO FREE BOOKS!**
♣	♣	♣	**Worth ONE FREE BOOK!**
🔔	🔔	🍒	**TRY AGAIN!**

www.eHarlequin.com

(H-AR-06/05)

DETACH AND MAIL CARD TODAY!

The Harlequin Reader Service® — Here's how it works:

Accepting your 2 free books and gift places you under no obligation to buy anything. You may keep the books and gift and return the shipping statement marked "cancel." If you do not cancel, about a month later we'll send you 4 additional books and bill you just $4.24 each in the U.S., or $4.99 each in Canada, plus 25¢ shipping & handling per book and applicable taxes if any.* That's the complete price and — compared to cover prices of $4.99 each in the U.S. and $5.99 each in Canada — it's quite a bargain! You may cancel at any time, but if you choose to continue, every month we'll send you 4 more books, which you may either purchase at the discount price or return to us and cancel your subscription.

*Terms and prices subject to change without notice. Sales tax applicable in N.Y. Canadian residents will be charged applicable provincial taxes and GST. Credit or debit balances in a customer's account(s) may be offset by any other outstanding balance owed by or to the customer.

after I've asked you to stop. Kagan is furious by what's been going on, and now he wants someone's blood. Unless I'm mistaken, he's going to remind me that there's a clause in my lease saying if I or any of my employees do anything to defame the management, my lease is null and void. So, like I said, you'll have to stop making waves, for both our sakes."

Lili stared at him. "And if I agree to stop, what about your part of the bargain?"

"I made you a promise to help," Tom said, relieved that she seemed to understand. "I always intended to keep my word to help you. I'd hoped you intended to keep yours."

"I was only doing what I thought was important," she answered. "As for us, what will your father think when he sees we no longer appear to be together?"

"He'll just have to find something else to keep him busy," Tom said with a conviction he didn't feel. Experience had taught him that, having envisioned Tom's future with Lili, his father would not take their apparent breakup lightly.

It had been a miracle the night Tom had discovered he cared for Lili. He would need another one to convince his father he'd made the right choice.

"I am not like you, Tom," Lili said after a moment's hesitation. "For you, your father's wishes are merely an annoyance. For me, as a woman raised by loving grandparents, I understand his wish to have grandchildren. Even if they would not be his biologically."

"Even after the twins showed their independent streak?"

"I think your father believes he could come to care for the twins when he gets to know them," Lili replied.

"You're probably right, but I'm not sure what to do about it." When Tom saw tears forming in Lili's eyes, his intentions to put her out of his life for her own good were shot to hell. No matter what Kagan thought, or what his father was trying to do, Tom wanted Lili. And not for just a night or two.

The only thing that kept him from taking her into his arms and apologizing was her reminder that his father was still trying to run his life. "I'm too old for this," Tom muttered. "Dad will just have to wait until I'm ready to start a family of my own."

"Then it is just as well that we part now," Lili answered slowly as she handed him back the crumpled summons. "The problem for me is not only the center. I do not wish to care for a man who is not ready for children. If the twins grow close to you and then lose you, they will suffer too much. They have already lost one man in their life. They do not need to lose another, even if it is only pretend."

Tom glanced around the studio to make sure they were still alone, then moved closer to Lili. Close enough to inhale her womanly scent and see the sweetness in her that lay beneath the surface. He might not have convinced Lili to knock off her crusade, but he was damned if he'd leave her without at least letting her know how sorry he felt at having hurt her.

"The next time I make love to you, Lili—and believe me when I tell you I intend to—you're going to love me back," he said softly. "And when I do make love to you, you'll know I'm loving you because I want to, not because of anything my father might want."

He drew a deep breath and mentally counted to ten. Even though he wanted to kiss away the furrow on

Lili's forehead, he had to put their lovemaking out of his mind, at least for now. "I do care for you, but I'm afraid it looks as if this isn't the right time for us."

Seeing the hurt in Lili's eyes damn near broke his heart. She might be a thorn in the side of Riverview's management, but she was *his* thorn. And, damn it all, in spite of what she might think of his trying to make her back down from her mission, the last thing he wanted was to have her turn into a meek "Sullivan Woman." Lili was a mixture of traditional woman and modern rebel. The kind who kept a man interested and on his toes.

"Lili, I only came here to tell you your part of the bargain is over. That we have to cool it for a while." Tom hoped she would understand the situation he found himself in. "I'm here on business this morning, but what goes on between us outside of the office is something else.

"Believe me," he added, trying to convince Lili as well as himself that there was a future for them. "All I'm really asking is that we put our relationship on hold for a while and that you stay out of trouble."

"No." Lili turned back to her drawing board. "I made a bargain to keep your father happy. I admire and respect him and intend to honor my part of the bargain. As for the day care center, I do not wish you to take over my responsibilities. As I have told you before, I am a grown woman and able to take care of myself."

Tom didn't need to be reminded that Lili was a grown woman, not after the night they'd spent together. The problem was, she was beginning to sound like his college sweetheart—too intent on doing things her way to realize she was only headed for trouble.

"Damn it, Lili! I'm trying to be sensible here. All I want to do is keep you out of harm's way until things settle down. You're not making it easy for me!"

When Lili didn't answer, Tom sensed he hadn't convinced her to back off. And from the glimmer of tears in her eyes, he knew he'd done a lousy job of making her believe he wasn't saying goodbye.

Still, he couldn't let her go without trying one more time.

"Okay, if my father and the day care are that important to you, I have another idea." He took a deep breath and plunged into a proposition that had come to him out of the blue. "How about we consider an engagement of convenience to keep everyone happy?" *Including, heaven help him, himself.* "That way, Kagan will hesitate to blame you."

Frowning, Lili turned back to him. "What is this 'engagement of convenience'?"

By now, Tom's thoughts were in such a turmoil, he wasn't sure just what he did mean. He'd coined the phrase, but he'd be damned if he knew how to go about creating such a thing.

What he did know was that because of his well-known no-fraternization policy and his 24-7 work schedule, no one would buy the idea he was involved with Lili unless he did something to make their relationship look real.

"What I had in mind was that we appear together more often, to pretend we're actually engaged," he managed to say. "I'll even buy you a ring, if you want." He didn't add that the idea of Lili wearing his ring was making him suddenly very happy.

From the look in Lili's eyes, she wasn't as thrilled by his scheme as he was.

"Pretend to be engaged? For how long?"

"For as long as it takes to get the center on solid footing. Maybe for another month or two. But first you've got to promise not to pull any more foolish stunts."

Lili frowned. "A month or two?"

"That's right. But don't forget, you have to promise to tell me if you come up with any new ideas for your crusade. Deal?"

From the thoughtful look on Lili's face, he was afraid the answer was no. He didn't blame her. Why would a woman with kids agree to such a sham?

But once the issue of the day care was resolved, Tom intended to start all over again and do his best to convince Lili they belonged together in a much more permanent way.

To his relief, she held out her hand to him. "As you say here in this country, a deal is a deal. But not before you explain what we must tell your father during this engagement of ours."

Tom winced. If he told his father he and Lili were engaged, he'd never hear the end of it. Still…

Tom shook Lili's hand. If Saturday night's romantic moments didn't have a way of flashing through his mind every time he gazed into her exotic eyes, keeping his focus on business would be easy.

"Trust me," he said, hearing voices coming down the hall. "We'll talk later." Tom had to fight the desire to kiss a smile back onto her lips. But if he gave in to the impulse to show her just how much she meant to him, she would never believe their relationship had to remain on a business footing for now. "How about tonight after work?" he suggested.

"I help the twins with their homework every night,"

she said with a hesitant smile. "If you would like to help, we can talk after the children go to sleep."

Tom was surprised that first grade kids had homework. He couldn't remember his own experience, but Megan's first grade education had included learning how to get along with other children, counting to a hundred, and taking daily naps to help her grow.

Recalling how mischievous Megan had been, Tom realized the naps might have been a way to help her teachers retain their sanity. Maybe things had changed.

"I have a better idea. Why don't I see if Megan can take the kids to a movie for a few hours so we can be alone?"

Lili shook her head. "I'm sorry, but homework is important. The twins have school tomorrow."

Tom glanced around to make sure they were still alone, then reached behind Lili to untie her apron. It looked as if discussing their new agreement would have to wait.

"The real problem here," he said, slowly sliding his hands over her waist, her hips, the curve of her breasts, "is that I want to spend as much time alone with you as possible."

"Me, too." Lili agreed shyly. "But if we are going to enter this engagement of convenience, we have to consider the children."

Tom realized he hadn't sounded like a man who liked children, and he was smart enough to realize that when it came to a choice between her children and a man—especially with unusual propositions—a woman like Lili would always put her children first.

"I *would* like the children to get to know you, especially Paul," Lili explained. "He is too quiet when you are around him. I think it is because I have told him he is the man of our house. I think he's afraid things might change. But I must be very sure my children are not hurt by what we do."

Tom swallowed hard. How could he not have realized that if he and Lili pretended to be engaged, the kids might feel threatened?

He took a deep breath. "Why don't we take this engagement one day at a time? I think it would be better if we handle the problem of raising funds for the center before we discuss our relationship."

Lili nodded. "Maybe it would be better if we think of ourselves as friends for now and let the future take care of itself?"

Friends? Tom thought as he regarded Lili. *No way!* One way or another, he intended to take their relationship beyond friendship when the right time came.

The voices in the hall grew louder, reminding Tom they were about to be joined by the magazine's photographer and his assistant. There was no way he wanted anyone to think he and Lili were a twosome before she promised to stay out of trouble.

"We have to talk about this later, Lili," he said quietly. "I'm in this mess as deep as you are."

Obviously upset, Lili muttered something in French as she took crayon pastels from a holder and tossed them on the drawing board. His thoughtless use of the word *mess* hadn't helped, he was sure. Just as well he didn't understand French. A glance back to Lili, who was staring at the blank sheet of drawing paper, wasn't reassuring.

As he left the studio, he eyed the samples of Lili's drawings that were pinned to the studio walls. The pastel sketches glowed with the same warmth and love of life as Lili herself—qualities Tom had tried without success to capture on canvas.

He walked away sensing that he was further away from truly understanding the real Lili than ever before.

Hell, all he was trying to do was keep her out of trouble. If it hadn't been for that stubborn streak of hers, he wouldn't have had to concoct this engagement of convenience.

He had to remind himself the magazine's lease depended on not antagonizing the owner. If he continued to employ anyone who defamed the Riverview or its management, the lease for *Today's World* could be terminated.

A chill ran over him.

Instead of waiting for an elevator, Tom took the stairs up to his office. He threw open the door to the landing and headed down the hall. Unless Lili changed her mind, he was on the verge of being a newly engaged man, if only for pretend.

Win, lose or draw, when this detour from sanity was over, he intended to make love to Lili until he drove both of them out of their minds. And then, by God, he'd make love to her all over again.

BACK IN THE STUDIO, Lili mulled over Tom's unusual offer. She wasn't sure what this engagement of convenience meant to him. As far as she was concerned, either a couple was engaged to be married or they were not.

Still, she'd made a commitment and she intended to keep it.

If Tom thought he'd persuaded her to keep a low profile, he was in for a surprise. Her pragmatic French up-bringing and the loss of the twins' father had made her stronger than even she realized.

Job or not, she would never back down from a prob-lem. Provided she stayed out of trouble, she didn't see any reason to do so now.

Besides, maybe she'd been wrong about Tom. Maybe he cared about her as deeply as she cared for him.

Her thoughts swung back to the original reason for their pretend relationship—Tom's father. If only their new bargain was not also meant to please a man whose influence Tom resented, she would have felt better about it.

In the meantime, she intended to quietly move on with her own plans. She needed to discuss them with April and Rita. Once they agreed to help her, she would take it from there.

Three heads were better than one.

She finished pinning drawing paper to her drafting table, picked up her pastels and went back to finishing her latest assignment with a vengeance—illustrating a travel article on Jamaica. She had no problem putting her heart and soul into the drawing.

First, she sketched a tropical beach where lazy waves caressed the shores. A beach whose warm white sands were lit up by the light of a full moon, waving palm trees, lovely sea grape and bougainvillea bushes.

She stood back and admired the scene, then realized something was missing. Carefully, she added a shower of stars overhead that would ultimately rain down on lovers.

At the edge of the beach, she sketched in the couple.

A petite blond woman in a skimpy two-piece bathing suit was held in the arms of a dark haired man with muscular shoulders. The lovers were embracing as if they never intended to part.

Every inch of Lili throbbed with empathy for the two lovers as their images emerged under her eager fingers. This was the honeymoon she'd fantasized for her and Tom.

Finally satisfied with her artistic efforts, she sat back and considered the finished sketch. By using the proper shading and pastels, she'd managed to carefully duplicate Tom's coloring and the striking features that had attracted her the first moment she'd met him. She'd used her own features and coloring for the woman.

When he saw her drawing, there would be no doubt in Tom's mind who the entwined lovers were meant to be. Just as there had been no doubt in her own mind from the moment she'd envisioned the setting that she and Tom belonged in it.

He would never be able to think of her as a mere convenience again.

One way or another, she intended to come up with an idea to bring them together for real.

Or her name wasn't Lili Soulé.

Chapter Ten

At lunch time, Lili told April and Rita about what had happened at the party Saturday night.

"I have found another way to raise money for the center." She giggled as she described how Tom had "suggested" to several of the male tenants that they should donate to her crusade.

"That's a setup for blackmail!" Rita looked admiringly at Lili. "Legal, maybe, but still blackmail!"

Lili shrugged. "Maybe so, but as you say here in this country, a woman has to do what she has to do."

Rita gave a congratulatory victory salute. "Now you're getting down and dirty! Run that story by me one more time!"

When someone as daring as Rita showed such enthusiasm over her plan, Lili began to feel a twinge of worry. Still, considering how excited Rita was at the idea, she was only too happy to comply.

"Anyway, as I have told you," Lili began, "it all started at the party Saturday night. Tom went to get some hors d'oeuvres. I was speaking to a few men when he came back. Before I knew what was happening, he spoke to the three and shamed them into leaving. But not before he made each of them promise to make a large contribution to the center!"

"How did he get the men to do it?"

Lili paused to think. Maybe this was what Rita had meant by blackmail. Just in case, Lili would keep the details to herself so they wouldn't come back to haunt her. As far as she was concerned, the means of getting the contributions didn't count as much as the results. "I am not sure exactly what Tom had in mind when he spoke to them," she said demurely, "but I remember there was some talk about wives, ex-wives and girl-friends."

Rita gazed at her admiringly. "It sounds as if Tom was jealous. I wouldn't have believed this cockamamy story of yours if I hadn't heard it straight from the horse's mouth. There is a problem, though. What if those guys change their minds? Coercing someone into making a large donation could get you arrested."

Lili felt herself blanch. She'd been so delighted with Tom's accomplishment she hadn't stopped to consider the possibility it might backfire. "Arrested? *Mon Dieu!*"

April threw an arm around Lili's shoulders. "*Mon Dieu* is right! Come on, Rita, there's no point in frightening Lili. Personally, I think I know the guys she's talking about. If I'm right, they've got it coming. Go on, Lili. Tell us how you came up with your new idea."

"It was from a story I saw on television where a man was 'persuaded' to help. I remembered shots were fired. Not that I think there will be any kind of violence this time." She shuddered. "I only want to raise enough money to keep the center open without the owner increasing everyone's rents."

Rita burst into laughter. "I'm willing to bet this won't

make Tom happy. From what you've said, he's already told you he wants to run the show by himself."

Lili glanced around to make sure no one was listening, then lowered her voice anyway. "I am not asking the men to make promises. I only hope to remind them to *keep* their promises."

"It doesn't really make a difference," Rita said with a wink. "Some men think it's cool to be macho, but it's up to women like us to be smart enough to use that against them. So, give. Are you trying to tell us Tom was jealous?"

Lili smiled shyly as she recalled the look on Tom's face when he'd found her surrounded by men. "Yes. That was a surprise to me, too."

"And all because of a complaint from the Riverview's management about those fliers," Rita crowed. "Well, I have to hand it to you, Lili. You've sure managed to make Tom notice you. I don't know what it's going to take to make him come up with a genuine proposal of marriage, but the way I look at it, making him jealous was a good start. Go on, what happened next?"

Lili blushed. "We left the party early to find someplace to talk things over."

"Talk? Privately?" Rita's eyes widened. "You're putting me on! If he was jealous when he saw men hitting on you, you're telling us all Tom wanted to do was talk?"

Lili nodded demurely. "Since Tom's sister was babysitting the twins at my house, he offered his place for this talk. Naturally," she added, "I took him up on his offer."

"Naturally," April echoed dryly. "Since it was Tom, I wouldn't have thought otherwise."

"Did I miss something here?" Rita asked. "It sounds to me as if you actually wanted to go home with him."

"What woman would not?" Lili blushed again as she recalled just how eagerly Tom had agreed to her suggestion that they go to his place instead of hers. Still, she would never reveal the details of how they'd wound up doing a great deal more than talking.

This time, Rita waved her arms in cheerleader fashion. "Atta girl!"

Lili smiled at her friend's approval. "Something told me Saturday night would be the right time and the right place to suggest going to Tom's," she said. "So naturally I did what any real woman would do. I bought a new black cocktail dress with a low neckline to here." She indicated a place midway down her breasts. "Tom's reaction was…" She blushed as she recalled just how he had reacted.

"Tom Eldridge reacting to a sexy dress?" April scoffed. "Not the Tom I know." "He's a real 'Sullivan guy.' I'm sure he wants a low-key woman, someone who thinks the way he does. You must have really done a number on him."

Lili blushed. "With a man like Tom, a woman like me has no choice. I had to do something to wake him up." She paused for effect. "And I did."

"Are you saying what I think you're saying?" Rita's voice quivered with excitement.

Lili blushed as she recalled making love with Tom. "All I am willing to say is that Saturday night turned out to be the most wonderful of my life."

Rita looked ready to burst. "Wow! And here *I've* been giving *you* lessons on how to get Tom's attention. I should have known Frenchwomen are born with the right instincts. Don't stop now, Lili. Tell us what happened next."

Lili couldn't resist smiling at the memory of just what *had* happened next. Even now she found it hard to believe the magical night she'd spent with Tom had actually happened. "We finally decided it was a good time to talk about how we really felt about each other."

"Only talk?" Rita teased. "Come on, Lili. You can't go this far without telling us everything."

April glanced through the glass partition to where Arthur, the office gofer, was approaching with his refreshment cart. She made for the door. "Hang on a minute. Don't say another word until I get back, Lili. And Rita, don't you push her. I don't want to miss hearing what Lili and Tom 'talked' about." She shot out of the office and down the hall to intercept Arthur.

"I guess I'm not the only one who would like to know how you managed to turn a guy like Tom into a human being like the rest of us," Rita said. "The way he acts around here, I figured he'd be an old man before some Delilah went the whole nine yards and seduced him."

"I am not this Delilah," Lili demurred, knowing she'd seen a side of Tom that no one else at the magazine had been allowed to see. "I would never ask him to become anyone else than the wonderful man he already is. He is a true gentleman," she added with a reminiscent smile at the memory of how gentlemanly Tom had been in their mutual seduction.

What she didn't say was that even though Tom had waited for her to make the first move, he had to have realized she'd wanted him as much as he'd wanted her.

What she wasn't prepared to tell her friends was that

their "talking" had taken place only after he'd finally driven her home the next morning.

"Maybe he is," Rita teased. "But even a gentleman can be made to see the light by the right woman."

"But first the woman has to do something to make the man realize she is the right woman for him, yes?"

"Yep," Rita said with a knowing smile. "It was that way with me and Colby, although I confess I let him think *he* caught *me*. So…did you or didn't you?"

"Did I what?" Lili asked innocently. How could she tell the whole story of what had happened without melting into a puddle like the fabled Wicked Witch of the West in the *Wizard of Oz?*

April hurried back into the office carrying three cups of black-as-sin coffee. "This ought to help keep us awake while you tell the whole story. I stopped Arthur before he had a chance to come in. I didn't want him to hear our conversation."

"Come on, Arthur's getting married in a couple of weeks," Rita said. "He can't be an innocent kid any-more——not if the Alice I know has her act together."

"Arthur and Alice are so lucky to have each other," Lili said wistfully. "I have already received an invitation to the wedding. For me, Tom has only offered an engagement of convenience. I do not think he will ever propose a real marriage, at least not to me."

"Hold on a minute!" April jumped up and hung a Do Not Disturb sign on the outside of her office door, then hurried back to sit on the edge of her chair. "What's this about an engagement of convenience?"

Lili glanced at her watch. "I am afraid it is too long a story. I have to go back to work."

"Then you'd better begin now." April motioned to the

closed door. "Go ahead, Lili. No one's coming in here unless I say so."

"Tom came to the studio to visit me this morning," Lili said. "He told me we should pretend to have an engagement—an engagement of convenience—to protect me."

Rita looked at her in horror. "A pretend engagement? Get outta here! After Saturday night?"

"Yes," Lili admitted. "But it took him only a few minutes to change his mind. He proposed an engagement of convenience for, he said, a couple of months to keep his father happy. At first I was hurt that he only wanted a temporary arrangement, but I agreed. And only because he promised to take over the fund-raising for the center."

She didn't add that, after Saturday night, she would have agreed to do almost anything he suggested.

Rita looked skeptical. "After the two of you spent all that time 'talking' things over, are you sure you understood that Tom didn't mean a real engagement?"

"I think so," Lili said. "But I didn't have time to ask him much before he left. I was too surprised by his offer."

"And to think that it all started with you getting yourself invited to Tom's place for this 'talk.'" Rita said admiringly. "That dress must have helped."

"It is the right of every woman to be admired, *non?*"

Rita nodded vigorously. "Absolutely! So, are you or aren't you engaged to be engaged?"

"I do not know." Lili sighed. "But that is not why I am here. I really came to tell you about the promise of contributions Saturday night and what I want to plan to do with them."

"I have to tell you I'm more fascinated with this engagement of yours than your fund-raising campaign," April said.

Lili shrugged. "The campaign is the most important thing. It does not matter if Tom and I get what we want out of our bargain. Maybe I am not the woman he wants, after all."

"Come off it, Lili! It doesn't take a rocket scientist to know that what you and Tom both want is each other—and for more than a couple of months. Especially after you've shown him how you feel about him."

And that she had done, Lili thought with a pleased smile. But some memories, especially those of Saturday night, were too precious to share.

As for Tom's attempts to make her promise to stay out of trouble, she hadn't really agreed. No matter what he said, she was ready to fight for what she believed in.

"You know, Lili," Rita said with a bright glint in her eyes, "it seems to me that this temporary engagement of yours might not be such a bum deal, after all. It shows that Tom cares for you, and he doesn't want you to get away from him."

"Right!" April chimed in. "So, as far as I can see, collecting from those guys is only fair. They crossed the line by coming on to you when you were Tom's date, and they ought to be made to pay for it. But let's get back to this new plan of yours, Lili."

April listened as Lili explained her new idea—based on Saturday night's events—to finance her crusade in spite of Tom's warning.

"Are you suggesting we go door-to-door in the building asking for contributions?" April asked when Lili had finished. "This is a twenty-story building!"

"I wasn't thinking of asking for contributions, exactly," Lili explained. "I was thinking more of a contest between the different floors. Each floor could come up their own idea. The floor that makes the most money wins a prize."

The more Lili explained her plan, the more excited she became. "I am sure there are many good ideas for a contest out there. We can put up a graph in the lobby showing how each floor is doing. The winning floor would get a grand prize and the loser a booby prize. What do you think?"

Rita whistled in approval. "Now *there's* a great idea! Next to gambling, people love a competition, especially if there's a prize for the winner. It's bound to get everyone fired up. How and when do we start?"

April looked worried. "Wait a minute! I know I sound like a wet blanket, but what makes you think Lili's plans won't rile Tom even more than he's riled up already? Or that Kagan will agree to the contest?"

"Because it will not cost him anything and it will make all the parents in the building happy," Lili explained.

"Sounds too good to be true," April muttered. "There have to be some drawbacks to the idea. I'm just afraid that if there is a flaw in there, Tom's smart enough to find it."

"Tom's opinion doesn't matter as long as I stay out of trouble," Lili answered, growing more and more pleased with herself and her idea. "As for the owner, from what Tom's father said about him, all Mr. Kagan worries about is the cost of keeping the center open. If Tom's father can't make the man agree to help us financially, my plan will take care of that."

What she didn't say was that she was worried about Tom's reaction to *any* plans she might come up with.

But she wouldn't change her mind. She had a mission to accomplish. "By the time Tom finds out what I'm planning, it will be too late for him to stop me!"

"Maybe so, but remember that you're supposed to keep a low profile," April warned.

"It doesn't matter," Lili said stubbornly. "I am tired of men thinking they are able to run things better than women. Just because I'm female does not mean I am helpless. Before I'm through, I intend to show Tom I am able to do many things without his help."

"Atta girl, now you're talking!" Rita said cheerfully. "Count me in! So now that we have that issue settled, why don't we let the games begin. April? How about you? Are you in?"

April hesitated. "To be honest, I don't know. I work closely with Tom. I'm afraid of what his reaction will be. What about you, Rita? You're *married* to a lawman. What do you think Colby will think of all this subterfuge?"

Rita wiggled her eyebrows. "Not to worry," she said smugly. "I might be a research librarian, but I don't want Colby to become bored with me. I intend to keep him guessing what I'll do next. Of course," she added modestly, "I *did* promise him I wouldn't hire any more airplanes, but that's all. Besides, I have an idea or two that will bring in tons of money. I volunteer to take on the magazine's two floors."

April frowned at Rita's enthusiasm. "That's what worries me. If I agree to help, there can't be any ideas that might set off Riverview's management again. I like my job and so does Lili. Agreed?"

"Agreed." Rita shrugged, but Lili knew from the lop-sided grin on her face that her friend wasn't fazed by the warning. "Like I said, I have a few interesting suggestions for the competition. So before you start to worry, I swear—everything will be on the up-and-up."

"Okay, then I'll go along, too," April said reluctantly, with a final warning look at Rita. "When and how do we start?"

Lili blew air kisses at Rita and April and headed for the door. "We'll have a planning meeting tomorrow at lunchtime in the cafeteria. In fact," she said with a happy smile, "I was so sure you would agree that I'm about to put a notice on the bulletin board before I go home."

JUST AS LILI WAS COVERING her drawing board, Tom strolled into the studio. "Reporting as requested. Ready?"

Puzzled, Lili paused. The last time she'd seen Tom, he'd declined to help the twins with their homework. "Ready for what?"

He paused to look at a proof the photographer's assistant was showing him for his approval. "Great, Joe. That's just what we need. Go ahead." He waved the man off and turned back to Lili. "You did say the twins need help with their homework, right?"

Lili glanced at their curious audience. "I thought you said you weren't interested in the children," she said in an undertone.

"Oh, I'm interested in the children, all right, although the truth is, I'm more interested in their mother," he assured her, making Lili blush. "I might not qualify as the world's best tutor, but I'm ready to do my part."

Bewildered by the change in Tom's attitude, Lili peered at him suspiciously. Never in her experience had a man kept her guessing the way Tom did. Nor had she ever met a man who was able to turn hot and cold almost on the hour. "Is this helping the twins with their homework part of this engagement of convenience?"

"Beats me. I've never really been engaged before." Tom shrugged and, to Lili's dismay, stole a glance at the work on her drafting table.

"I'm willing to admit I proposed the idea on impulse," Tom stated, apparently satisfied she hadn't been working on another flier, "but I'm not worried. Sooner or later I'm bound to figure out what I meant when I suggested it."

Lili's suspicions were confirmed. Instead of enjoying the twins, Tom intended to keep an eye on her, one way or another.

"And this helping the twins with their homework will help you decide?"

"You want the truth?"

"Always." Tom's approving glance swept over her, and there was a warm look in his eyes. There was no way she could think straight if he kept gazing at her as if he wanted to make love to her.

She had to remember their new agreement was still, as Rita had pointed out, pretend. Her good behavior in return for his cooperation.

"Something my sister said the other night helped change my mind," Tom told her. "Megan's convinced me that helping the kids with their homework would not only let Paul get to know me better, it would give you a chance to get to know me better, too."

Lili swallowed the lump in her throat. How much

better could she get to know him after spending a night together? "You really want to do this?"

"Whatever it takes," he said, moving closer until she could see the rapid pulse in his throat and, heaven help her, feel his body heat. "How else am I ever going to be able to finish that portrait of you?"

Ah, the portrait, Lili thought. It was true Tom didn't know her, she mused sadly. Otherwise he would have realized that the look in her eyes when he'd painted her had been one of love. No way would she have slept with him if she didn't care deeply for him.

Tom caressed her cheek with his thumb, ran his fingers over her lips, her chin. Her body warmed as she fought the impulse to press her lips into his hand, to step into his arms and kiss him back, this man who had won her heart.

Even as the woman in her thrilled to Tom's touch, the mother in her rebelled against the thought he might be using her children for his own ends. She wanted to tell him so, but decided to view his offer to help with the twins' homework as a challenge, one she intended to take him up on.

Still, she had to set out ground rules for their strange relationship.

If only she weren't so caught up in the heated look in his eyes, she would demand an explanation of just what he actually had in mind.

Chapter Eleven

Tom was aware Lili was surprised by his change of heart, but he figured he had to keep an eye on her. Not 24-7, maybe, but at least during their waking hours. If that included helping the twins with their homework, so be it.

Unfortunately, Lili wasn't talking as he drove her home. She was obviously either ticked off at him or trying to decide why he'd changed his mind.

After an enlightening telephone conversation with Mrs. London in the center, he'd learned counting to one hundred was, to his surprise, a big deal. Actually, Mary had told him, learning to count that high was an important mark of proficiency in the elementary school curriculum. Kids learned more than counting in the process, she'd told him. They learned odd and even numbers, graphing data, number patterns and reading the calendar, to add and to subtract and more other skills than he remembered.

He was pretty sure that even if the twins already knew these things, they didn't realize what being able to utilize numbers could do for them. At least when it came to handling money. With finance his particular specialty since he'd taken over the magazine, he was ready to get them going.

Glancing through the rearview mirror, he saw a frown on Paul's face and, surprise surprise, he was holding his sister's hand. Apparently the boy really did feel threatened by Tom's appearance in their lives.

One thing for sure, Tom told himself as he pulled up in front of their house, it was up to him to turn the frown into a smile. All he had to do was take his sister's advice: relax and try to have fun.

He trailed Lili and the kids to the front door, hoping that the bright idea he'd come up with would make a difference in his relationship with the twins. Merely helping with dreaded homework wasn't going to cut it.

Paul stopped in his tracks. "What's that funny noise?"

Tom figured that appealing to the kid's innate curiosity had to be a good start. He put his hands in his pants pockets to still the sound that had caught Paul's attention.

"Let's go inside and I'll show you."

"I should have told you we are having take-out pizza for dinner tonight," Lili said as she took off her jacket and helped the twins with their backpacks. "I hope that is all right with you. For now, there is milk and the brownies I baked last night for a snack while the children do their homework."

Given that all he could think of was how attractive Lili looked tonight, Tom took the homework reminder to heart. He had to concentrate on why he was here.

But homework was only one part of it.

From the calculating way the twins were looking at him, Tom felt like a magician up against a skeptical audience. If he intended to make friends with the kids, it was time to produce.

"Fine with me, providing I get a brownie," he said as he rubbed his stomach. "I'm starved." When Paulette giggled, he hid a grin and, trailed by the twins, led the way to the kitchen table to empty his pockets. Paulette, her eyes sparkling with interest, followed every move he made.

Not to be outdone, Paul sidled up to the table and stared as pennies poured from Tom's hand. Out of the corner of his eye, Tom saw signs of dawning interest on the boy's face.

"What are you going to do with those pennies?"

Gotcha!

"Hang on a minute." Tom took a bundle of bank penny wrappers from his jacket pocket and deposited them alongside the coins.

"Homework first!" Lili called from where she was pouring three glasses of milk and setting out a plate of brownies. "Mr. Eldridge can wait. You can play later."

"We don't have any homework tonight," Paul called back. "We just have to read a chapter in Dr. Seuss's book." He eyed the mound of pennies. "What are you going to do with these, Mr. Eldridge?"

Tom was prepared. "First we're going to count them, putting them in stacks of ten each until we get fifty. After that, we'll turn them into dollar bills."

Paulette's eyes widened as she studied the mound of pennies. "You really know how to do that?"

Tom figured he finally had Paulette's undivided attention. Now all he had to do was snare her brother. "Yep," he said casually. "Ready?"

Lili put the milk and brownies on the table and stood beside Tom to watch what he was doing.

He motioned to the coins. "Go ahead. Count out the pennies until you have stacks of ten. Do it five times." In short order the twins had the stacks ready. "Okay. How much money do you have?"

"That's easy," Paul said, as if anyone should have known the answer. "Fifty cents."

"Right," Tom agreed. "Now, if you take away ten pennies, how much do you have?"

Paulette hesitated while she counted on her fingers, but her brother answered promptly. "Forty cents."

"And if you add five?"

"Forty-five." Paul looked unimpressed. "That's no big deal. I thought you were going to show us how you turn the pennies into dollar bills!"

"Sure thing," Tom answered. "Just go back to stacking the pennies into stacks of ten each and I'll show you."

Lili moved closer to Tom. "You should not try to fool the children," she whispered in his ear. Instead of feeling admonished, Tom was aware of a sharp longing shimmying through him at Lili's husky admonition. If they'd been alone, he would have taken her in his arms and given in to the urge to kiss her.

Instead, he pretended innocence. "What makes you think I'm kidding?"

"Because no one can change coins into dollar bills," she answered as she watched the twins busily piling pennies into neat little stacks of ten each.

Tom reached for a brownie and took a bite. "Stick around and I'll show you I'm right."

When the twins finished counting out their piles of pennies, Tom helped them insert the coins into the penny wrappers he'd brought with him. "There," he said as he folded down the ends of the wrappers.

"Those aren't dollar bills," Paul complained. "I knew you couldn't do it!"

"Sure they are. All you have to do is go to the bank and trade two wrapped stacks for a dollar bill."

"That's it?" Paul frowned. "That's not a real trick," he grumbled. "*You* were supposed to turn the pennies into dollars!"

"No problem." Tom waved his hand, then carefully produced the dollar bills he'd hidden up his sleeve. "There you go."

Paul took his but he didn't look convinced. "Now what happens to the coins?"

Tom put the wrapped coins in his pocket. "No problem. I'll take them to the bank. All you have to do is enjoy your dollar."

Wide-eyed, Paulette clutched her prize to her chest. "Can I spend it?"

"If you want to," Tom said, "but maybe it would be a better idea to open a bank account and let your money earn interest. Who knows when another dollar bill might turn up?"

Her brother shot him a knowing look that told Tom he was not only on to him, but smart enough to know what Tom was up to. And that it hadn't been a lesson in counting or adding and subtracting, either.

Thank God the kid had a sense of humor, Tom thought as he gratefully acknowledged Paul's look with a nod. Maybe children weren't as hard to please as he'd thought. With a handful of coins, he'd managed to take the first step in establishing a man-to-man bond with Paul. Bonding with athletic Paulette would be a different story.

Lili stared dubiously at Tom as the children went to

work on the milk and brownies. "This is helping the children with their homework?"

As if the lesson in arithmetic had been an everyday occurrence, Tom nodded casually. "Sure. The kids have practiced how to count by tens, do some simple addition and subtraction, and, hopefully, learned about saving money. All that's left is for you to take the kids to the bank and help them open a savings account. As a matter of fact—" he winked at Paulette "—I'll bet when they see their bank balances grow, they might be more interested in saving money instead of spending it."

Judging from the doubtful look on Paulette's face, Tom wasn't prepared to bet she'd be willing to open a bank account anytime soon.

Lili didn't look convinced, either. "That is all?"

"Sure. As far as I'm concerned, the lesson on finance was as much a valuable bit of education as reading. At least, that's what one of my teachers told me."

Lili eyed him as if he'd lost his mind. And she was right, Tom thought. He had. But not over arithmetic. He'd lost his mind over her. Still, her guarded expression told him that if this was what he'd meant by helping the twins with their homework, he was out of luck.

When Lili picked up the empty milk glasses and plate, Tom tried a friendly smile. Sensing her skepticism at his novel approach to homework, he figured the kids must have inherited their sense of humor from their father.

"Go and clean up for dinner, children," Lili said with a telling look at Tom. "I wish to speak to Mr. Eldridge alone for a few minutes."

When the twins hesitated, Tom said, "Go ahead. If you like, I'll listen to you read Dr. Seuss after dinner. I take it I'm invited?"

Lili shot him an annoyed glance, but she didn't say no.

He might be in trouble with their mother for the moment, but at least the kids looked a little friendlier than they had a short time ago. "All I intended to do was make learning simple addition and subtraction into a fun game. It worked, didn't it?"

"With the twins, perhaps, but not with me." Lili put the empty glasses in the sink, motioned him into a chair and sat down across the table from him. "I do not like surprises," she said softly. "Even though I invited you here tonight, I am also not comfortable with the way you keep coming up with strange ways to bring us together. If this is part of this engagement of convenience, I think we need to talk."

"Sure, you go first." Tom reached for Lili's hand and brought it to his lips before she could pull away. The rich scent of chocolate that mingled with the clean smell of soapy water was as potent as any perfume and, considering their proximity, just as exciting. "All I ask is that you agree to let me take care of the center."

Lili pulled her hand out of his. "If we are to appear to be engaged, I need to know what you plan on doing next."

Tom glanced over his shoulder to make sure the twins hadn't come back, then took her hand again. "I'm playing it by ear, but yes, I'll tell you what I'm planning if you tell me what you're doing. Anyway, like I said, for now the engagement is largely for Dad's sake."

"Have you told him about us?"

"Not yet, but I will," Tom promised.

"And this engagement is not for us?"

Caught by the questioning look in Lili's eyes, Tom felt as if he'd been hit by a whirlwind of emotions.

After seeing her at home with the twins, he was more certain than ever that she was the nesting kind. And he wasn't sure he was ready to face everything that came with being a father. Not yet.

The truth was that while he wanted Lili in all the ways a man wanted a woman, he wasn't any more sure about the kids than they were about him.

So, he thought regretfully, the engagement had to be, at least for the next few months, a fictitious one.

Now it appeared that his real problem was to persuade Lili to join him in pretending.

"Two months, Lili," he said softly. "Until then, maybe there's no need to set any rules, after all. Let's just play our relationship by ear while I do what I can to save the day care. We can do all the talking we want later."

He punctuated his remarks by kissing the inside of her wrist. "I'm looking forward to the time when talking about rules and promises won't be necessary anymore. When we can explore how we really feel about each other."

Lili's eyes widened at Tom's attempt to explain the engagement. An explanation that was really no explanation at all, she thought. The promise of a renewed personal relationship should have taken her senses by storm. But how could it when she wasn't sure just what Tom was promising?

A delicious shiver ran through her as she recalled what it was like to be in Tom's embrace. Those arms that had held her close and closer still until she hadn't been able to think—only to feel. And to believe, through a haze of desire, that she had found her true soul mate.

She swallowed a sigh. Whether she liked it or not,

the more immediate problem facing her was not if and when she and Tom would relive those magical moments. What she had to do was find a way to put her own plans into action. Plans that no longer could include fliers and petitions.

What she *did* have in mind was bound to satisfy even the most critical of property owners like Kagan.

"No more rules? No more promises?" she asked Tom as she looked into his eyes, wishing she could believe the promise she thought she saw there. "Or is this another game of yours simply to silence me?"

"Yes, in answer to your first two questions, and no to the third." Tom went on to kiss his way to her elbow. Despite knowing the children were nearby, she could barely keep herself from leaning into his arms and making a full confession of her plans. "Truce?"

As his moist, brownie-laced breath caressed her sensitive skin, Lili felt she would surely melt. She found it hard to believe that the greater the emotional distance she tried to put between herself and Tom, the closer they seemed to become.

When Tom raised his head at her silence, she put her heart and soul into a smile.

"As you say, truce."

IN RESPONSE TO THE NOTICE she'd posted on the bulletin board, the Riverview's cafeteria was humming with excitement. When Lili walked in, people forgot their lunch and stood up and cheered. The servers behind the counters clapped.

Lili took a quick glance around the cafeteria to make sure Tom wasn't there. She knew it might be only a matter of time before he heard about her plans, but she intended to act before he tried to stop her.

In the meantime, and to her growing delight, the contest to see which floor could raise the most money to save the center seemed to have caught everyone's attention. Even the three men from the party, who apparently felt obligated to be there.

Backed up by April and Rita, Lili smiled her thanks and made her way through her cheering audience to the back of the room, where she climbed onto a chair.

"Thank you all for coming here today," she said when the noise finally wound down. "Since I know you are already aware of the problem of keeping our children's center open, I think we can go directly to each floor's suggestions for a contest."

Another round of cheers brought a blush to her cheeks. She'd never wanted or expected to be anyone's heroine, but felt good knowing she was being instrumental in helping other parents in the same position as she was.

"I'm afraid it will take more than one meeting to plan the contest," she said with a wide smile. "But for now, I will call on a representative from each floor to tell us what ideas you have come up with. We start at the top floor, no?"

"We start at the top, yes." To Lili's surprise, Theo Mecouri, the manager of the penthouse restaurant, stood. "Although we're part of management, we also consider ourselves to be a part of the building's family."

Mecouri waited for new cheers to die down before he continued. "Our suggestion is that we sponsor a baking contest with an entry fee of ten dollars. The contest is to be open to any individual throughout the building instead of any one floor. For a prize, we will offer a catered dinner for four for the first-place winner. Of course," he added modestly, "we hope someone on our own staff will win."

April poked Lili in the ribs. "I'll bet Theo plans to have his pastry chef enter his chocolate soufflé. Go ahead, Lili, ask him if we get to eat the entries after the contest is over."

Aware of April's appetite for her favorite dessert, Lili obliged. To an outburst of laughter, she asked if April could buy Mecouri's entry when the contest was over.

"Sure. Entries will be for sale." Theo sent an amused look at April. "That should bring in extra funds."

Lili made a note on the tablet she was holding. "Thank you, Mr. Mecouri. Next, please."

To her surprise, Rick Hayes, the travel agency owner with a wandering eye who had hit on her at the party, stood up. "Instead of entering the contest, the sixth floor will contribute the grand prize—a fully paid weekend for two in New York City, courtesy of my agency." He waited until the applause died down. "I assume this will discharge my obligations?" he added with a meaningful glance at Lili.

Only too happy to accept the offer to pay up and forget, Lili made another note on her tablet. "That is wonderful, Mr. Hayes. I am sure everyone here thanks you for your generosity."

Apparently encouraged by Hayes's offer to get himself off the hook, Renaldo Perez, the wholesale jeweler, raised his hand. "I'll donate a gold necklace with a diamond drop for one of the prizes. That should take care of the second floor, right?"

Surprised by his appearance in the cafeteria and re-lieved that he had satisfied his obligations, Lili nodded and added another annotation on her notepad. "That would be wonderful. I'm sure everyone here thanks you, too," she exclaimed.

Pete Borden, the CEO of the advertising agency on the ninth floor, stood up. "My agency is offering to help advertise the contest. Of course," he quickly explained when someone hooted, "we'll cover all costs."

Lili held up her hand. "Thank you, but we are still in the planning stage. I will let you know when we need you."

Borden shrugged and sat down.

"Now," Lili stated, "I think we need to find a way to raise a large amount of money as soon as possible. Are there any other ideas?"

"There's mine!" Rita raised her hand and jumped to her feet. "I propose to auction a date with a bachelor as *Today's World*'s contribution for the ninth and tenth floors. Of course, the guy has to be a bachelor or it's not going to be any fun for the person who wins the bid. Right?"

A woman in the front of the room raised her hand. "Count me in. I'll make the first bid even without know-ing who's the guy!"

Everyone laughed at the comment by Noreen Talbot, the building's flamboyant first floor receptionist, as Lili added the suggestion to the list.

She didn't like the speculative way Rita was eyeing her, though. It didn't take a stretch of imagination to know why. Rita was imagining Tom as the bachelor to be auctioned.

"Thank you, Noreen!" she said. "As soon as Rita

comes up with a willing man, I will make sure you get the first chance to bid on him."

Below her, Lili heard Rita muttering. Her friend must have intended Lili to win Tom at the auction. Well, no matter. For better or worse, at least for the next two months, Tom was hers.

"Anyone else?"

"Yeah." A man in the back of the room stood up. "My name is Carlos Ruiz. I'm the owner of the employment agency on the fourth floor. I have another suggestion. How about if we auction off a date with a woman?"

This time, instead of cheers, there were boos from the females in the room.

"Sheesh," Ruiz said with a comical leer. "I didn't mean anything bad. It's only for a date. Besides, if a woman can bid on a guy, a guy ought to be able to bid on a woman. What's fair is fair."

"Okay, mister." Noreen Talbot stood up again. "If no one else volunteers to be the woman, I'll do it. But it's going to cost you!" She laughed when Ruiz made a face and sat down.

Another hand went up. "Floor number eight would like to run a rummage sale in the basement parking garage."

Lili held her pen poised above the tablet. "A rummage sale?"

"Sure, I'll bet there's a lot of people with stuff they don't use anymore. And just as many people needing the same kind of stuff—you know, clothes and things."

Lili nodded. "And your name and floor?"

"Rebecca Halstead. I'm an accountant with Schneer and Sons. I've done this before and I've always made several thousand dollars. With the number of people working in this building contributing their used books and clothing, I don't see why I can't do it again."

"Good," Lili replied with a grateful smile. "We will have to get management's permission to use the garage area, but not just yet. Anyone else?"

Mary London raised her hand. "I realize you might not want to do this because of financial reasons, but I think it might be a good idea to auction off a month's fees for child care."

Lili made another annotation. "Thank you, Mary, but I'm afraid that will depend on how much money we raise. Anyone else?"

"How about a block party? We can charge ten dollars a head."

Carlos Ruiz, the guy who had suggested they auction off a date with a woman, hooted. "A block party? How ya going to do something like that in the building? Unless…" He hesitated for a minute, then brightened. "Maybe we could hold it over in Navy Pier and charge admission?"

Lili tried, without luck, to stem the wave of excited comments before things got out of hand.

Rita climbed on another chair, put two fingers in between her lips and whistled. "Come on, people. Let's let Lili finish up here."

"I think a block party is a good idea," Lili agreed when the noise died down, "but it will take some planning. Maybe a committee, Carlos?"

"If that's what you want, sure, but, hey, it'll be a breeze. Maybe we can hold it on the roof of the parking structure. My wife and I have put together block parties before. All it takes is hamburgers and hot dogs, a lively band and lots of beer to help everyone loosen up." That remark brought on a renewed burst of laughter. "I'll even get my brother-in-law to donate a flat screen television for a raffle. He owns an appliance store."

Lili was pleased and surprised at the wonderful way her idea for a contest was going. "Thank you, Carlos and everyone else." She glanced at the large clock on the wall, and saw that the lunch hour was over. "I'm afraid we'll have to have another meeting tomorrow to finish up. Please remember that I would like to keep all the ideas low-key until we have most of our plans in place. Not that it's a secret, but if we can convince management they have nothing to lose and everything to gain, I am sure we will be allowed to proceed."

Before the management's meeting that might seal the center's fate, Lili thought as she accepted congratulations.

And if Tom didn't hear about the contest before she told him herself.

Chapter Twelve

"You're planning on doing what?"

Lili could only stare at Tom, her insides turning somersaults at the shocked expression on his face.

A moment ago, there'd been a welcoming smile there. Now the smile had faded and a wintry look replaced it.

She had only herself to blame.

After a struggle, she'd decided to tell Tom about the contest before he found out for himself. After all, he'd asked her to clue him in on her plans, and she'd agreed, hadn't she? But she'd never seen him this worked up, not even on the day he'd caught her making that incriminating flier.

Not even when Paulette had inadvertently kicked a soccer ball into his groin.

And not even when he'd found three men hitting on her.

If he'd been upset before, he was furious now.

Knowing how strongly he felt about her involvement to save the center, maybe she should never have told him about the contest, but let him find out for himself.

"Don't just stop there," he said in a voice that should have sent her skittering out the door. "Since you've gone this far, you might as well go ahead and give me the whole story."

Now that she'd opened the door to trouble, Lili felt she had no choice but to go through. And to trust that Tom would be more reasonable when he heard her out.

She eyed him warily. "We are planning a floor-by-floor contest throughout the building to see which one can raise the most money for the center."

"Let me guess," Tom said as he rose and came around his desk. "The 'we' in all of this is you again."

She swallowed the lump in her throat and took another small step closer to the door. "Yes."

He followed her. "What kind of contest?"

Lili stalled for time by pretending to consult the small notebook she'd brought with her. The notations she'd made about the individual fund-raising offers that had thrilled her before somehow didn't seem so exciting anymore.

Unfortunately, there was no way she could climb out of the hole she'd dug for herself. She would have to "go for broke"—one of Rita's favorite expressions—and hope that the better side of Tom would take over.

She took a deep breath and read the rest of the suggestions for the contests.

"Of all the harebrained ideas you've come up with, Lili, I have to tell you this one's over the top." He broke in before she could tell him the list wasn't complete. "I thought you understood why I asked you to back off."

Lili's heart, already racing in a rapid two-step, broke into a polka. Thank goodness she hadn't had time to read him the whole list or he really would have hit the roof. Not that it mattered. The man glaring at her wasn't the one she'd thought she knew.

"Bake sales and rummage sales and block parties aside…" Tom finally muttered, "hell, they might be harmless. But did you ever stop to consider how the building's management might react once they hear you're thinking of pulling a fool stunt like auctioning off a man?" He paused as a thought struck him. "Who's the poor sucker you're going to auction off?"

Lili wasn't about to tell him which sucker Rita had in mind. Or that the auction hadn't been Lili's idea. And certainly not that someone had suggested auctioning off a woman. Not today, and from the look she saw in Tom's eyes, maybe never.

What he might do if he knew or even suspected *he* was Rita's target for the bachelor auction was too fearsome even to think about.

She recalled a favorite saying of her grandmother's: "there's a time and place for everything."

This was obviously not the right time to tell Tom anything more.

"I've tried to be up front with you and all I get for this honesty is your temper?" she protested. "I thought if I told you what I had planned, you would be proud of me."

"Oh, I'm proud that you take the time to think, all right," he said, staring at her as if he were seeing her for the first time. "I'm just not too happy with what you're thinking about. I wish you'd stopped to consider the position you put me in with the building's management before you went this far. The last thing I need is for them to think I can't control my own staff."

Considering the way he was glaring at her, Lili decided that trading on Tom's better nature wasn't going to get her anywhere. On the other hand, as her grandfather had often told her when she was growing up, a strong offense was better than a weak defense.

"What happened to your 'no more rules' and 'no more promises' offer?" she asked, trying to be indignant, when every nerve in her body was quivering with anxiety. "If those were only words to keep me quiet, they aren't going to work. I have never been a meek woman and I am not about to start now! Not even for this engagement of convenience of yours!"

"Meek? Ha!" Tom accused. "You're the most stubborn, single-minded woman I've ever met! What about *your* promises? I distinctly remember you agreed to let me take care of fund-raising while you stayed out of trouble!"

"*Non!* I may have agreed to *try* to stay out of trouble, but I remember only agreeing to a truce! A truce," she added with a blush she knew gave herself away, "that we sealed with a kiss!"

Instead of answering, Tom shrugged and turned back to his desk. "I guess I should be grateful you're not out there circulating petitions," he muttered. "Or are you?"

Lili shook her head.

"Good. And as for a contest involving the entire building, if that's your idea of a truce, I'd hate to think of what you might have come up with if we didn't have one."

Lili bit her lower lip. She wasn't going to give up until she had to. And maybe not even then. Still, she figured that since they *were* supposedly engaged, she had nothing to lose by confiding in Tom and getting his assurance he wouldn't interfere with her plans. What would happen after he discovered that *he* was Rita's choice for the auction was something she refused to contemplate.

"Are you saying we must not have this contest?"

"No, I'm not," he answered with a bitter look. "Hell, I don't seem to have any control over my own employees, let alone the entire building." He gestured to the pile of papers on his desk. "We'll have to talk about this later. Right now I have some work I have to get ready for my accountant. Since Arthur is out sick today, what do you say we continue this conversation over coffee in the cafeteria. Say, in about an hour?"

Lili smothered a gasp. She'd been honest about no more fliers or petitions. But if Tom saw the notice for the planning meeting she'd just pinned to the cafeteria's bulletin board, truce or not, he'd fire her for sure. At the moment she needed her job more than she needed his approval.

"Thank you, but I do not drink coffee," she said proudly. "Besides, I have my own work to finish this morning." Without waiting for his reply, she rushed out the door.

LILI HEADED FOR THE magazine's library. After hearing what Tom thought of the idea for a bachelor auction, she had to stop Rita.

"Thank goodness you're here," Lili said breathlessly when her friend looked up from her computer. "We must talk!"

"I think you'd better sit down and take a deep breath before you collapse." Rita motioned to the chair beside her desk and waited until Lili's breathing returned to normal. "What's up?"

Lili put her hand over her wildly beating heart. "I told Tom about the contest and he hit the roof!"

Rita frowned. "You didn't happen to include my bachelor auction idea, or did you?" She held up a staying hand. "No, you don't have to answer. I can tell you did. Frankly, you look a mess."

"Yes," Lili gasped, brushing her hair out of her eyes. "I couldn't wait for an elevator so I ran down the stairs. It's just that I made the mistake of thinking Tom should know of my plans before he heard them from someone else."

"Sheesh," Rita retorted. "Tom's the last man I'd take into my confidence at this stage of the game."

"Then how did you intend to get him to agree to be auctioned off?"

Rita grinned. "By trading on his male ego, that's how. I'm not sure if you know it, Lili, but men are ninety percent ego. Once the word gets out that Tom's up for bid, he'll be too flattered at the attention to even think about backing out."

Lili wasn't so sure. After the scene in his office, she wasn't convinced he could be flattered, and definitely not about his sexuality. "You are sure? Even your own Colby?"

"Trust me." Rita laughed. "Texas Rangers have a reputation for being tough, but under that sexy uniform beats a typical male heart. How do you think I caught the guy?"

Lili blushed. "I understood that you saved his life! How could he not have fallen in love with you?"

"Don't tell Colby you think I saved him, for heaven's sakes," Rita said with a wry glance at her wedding ring. "I have him convinced he was saving me! As for you, Lili, I'm sure you've heard of the old American saying, 'A woman's gotta do what she's gotta do.'"

Lili jumped to her feet. "Yes," she agreed as she made for the door. "Right now I have to go down to the cafeteria and take down the notice of another meeting today before Tom sees it. Whatever plans I still have to make for this contest are going to be private from now on! But first—" she paused at the door "—you must forget your plan to use Tom for the bachelor auction."

Rita shrugged, and Lili had a sinking feeling that, as always, her friend would do what she wanted to do.

TOM STARED THROUGH the glass partition at Lili's disappearing figure as she rushed to the stairwell, obviously too distraught to wait for the elevator. She didn't drink coffee? Like hell she didn't—he'd seen her drink coffee, including refills, more than once. Maybe he'd missed something during their conversation.

It didn't take much to realize she was up to more than she'd told him about. Not a good omen for the future.

Work forgotten, Tom leaned back in his chair, folded his arms behind his head and contemplated the ceiling. Of all the women he'd come across, Lili had to be the last he would have expected to be a rebel. Not when it was her sweet, gentle manner and ethereal beauty that had attracted him long before he'd even admitted it to himself.

The change in Lili from a mild-mannered woman to a seductive siren and then a passionate crusader was driving him to distraction. She was three different women rolled into one unpredictable and beautiful package. No wonder he couldn't capture the real Lili on canvas.

Where had the woman he'd fallen in love with gone? The ceiling held no answers.

His thoughts turned to his friend Lucas. Of all the men he knew, his old fraternity brother was the last he would have imagined to come up with rules advising women on how to play the mating game. And then he'd changed his mind and married April Morgan, his chief critic.

Tom compared Lili with the list of "Sullivan's Rules."

Make her man feel masculine.

Well, he thought with a rueful grin, he couldn't complain about that one. Lili had been damn good at making him feel like a man. She deserved an A+ for that.

Sexual intimacy mustn't occur too soon.

Thank God, Lili believed sexual intimacy was a desirable part of their unusual relationship. Up until today, he would have given her an A++ for that one.

A woman must rein in her own desires to promote the health of a relationship. No way! He'd loved the way Lili's desires had matched his own. Another A++. Maybe even a triple A.

A woman must strive for compatibility as well as be sexy.

Well, he thought, he'd definitely give her an A for the sexy part of the rule. Compatibility, on the other hand, got a D.

Shower a man with affection and sublimate her own daily frustrations.

Not today. He gave Lili a D- for that one.

A woman must be supportive, fun-loving, easygoing, and generous in her praise of a man's achievements.

He had to stop to think about that one. Lili was supportive, fun-loving and generous in her praise, but definitely not easygoing—at least not lately. Add to that damn difficult to figure out. Grudgingly, he gave her a C for that rule.

Now that he was finished, he realized he was back where he'd started when he'd tried to analyze the complex woman he'd fallen in love with. Square one and no place to go from there. Not without some help.

He hadn't talked much about life—or women—with his father since he'd been a teenager about to go off to college, he thought with a heartfelt sigh. Even then his dad's advice hadn't taken root in Tom's psyche, or he wouldn't have ended up proposing marriage to the classmate he'd been dating.

His girlfriend had been an independent woman who, when the chips were down, hadn't been willing to settle for an unexciting life as his wife. With barely a good-bye, she'd headed for the bright lights of New York City. The letdown had been tough, but now that he'd found Lili, he realized he'd been damn lucky to be dumped.

What he did need was to talk to someone who had enough experience to help him get his head together. Since Lucas had written an article about women, surely he would know *something* more about them than Tom did. The last time they'd talked, Lucas had had a smile on his face. The guy might be an academic with his head in the clouds, but he'd still managed to talk April Morgan, the magazine's feisty editor, into marrying him. If Lucas could perform that miracle, by God, so could Tom.

It was time to call Lucas for another talk over a pint of ale.

Tom reached for the phone.

PADDY'S IRISH PUB had to be the perfect place for a heart-to-heart on the subject of what made women tick, Tom thought as he made his way to a corner booth located at the back of the room. The dim lighting, the rumble of male voices and the scent of good, strong Irish brew combined to create a place where a man could bare his soul to an old fraternity brother and possibly find some answers to the man-woman thing.

Not that he was a regular here. He hadn't been in Paddy's since he'd taken over the management of *Today's World*. Maybe that was the root of his problem; he'd been taking life too seriously.

It was definitely time for a change, but the question was should that change include Lili?

He took a deep swallow of ale just as Lucas came through the door. Tom stood and waved him over. "Glad you could make it," he said as they shook hands. "I hope April didn't mind my taking you away from her tonight?"

Lucas dropped into the seat. "No problem," he said with a broad smile. "April's out, too."

"Girls' night out?" Tom asked.

Lucas nodded and looked around for a waiter. "April's off at some kind of secret meeting—no husbands allowed. She didn't tell me what the meeting's about—treated it as some big mystery."

Tom frowned into his glass of ale. "She's probably out there fomenting more trouble with Rita and Lili."

Lucas laughed, waved to the waiter and pointed to Tom's drink. "I'll have the same," he called. He paused to take a close look at the scowl on Tom's face. "Better bring another for my friend here while you're at it." When the waiter waved back and drifted to the bar,

Lucas went on. "So, what kind of trouble are we talking about here?"

In between bouts of Lucas's laughter, Tom filled his friend in on Lili's latest crusade and its possible repercussions. "It's not the contest that bothers me as much as Lili herself. I don't think the management would complain about a bake sale or a rummage sale or a party in the parking area, but she hasn't stopped there. She's talking about auctioning off a man! You can imagine what a liability issue that could be. The building management would have a fit!"

Tom raked his fingers through his hair. "I used to think Lili was a reasonable woman. I have to tell you that she's about to drive me nuts. Maybe it's my fault. Maybe I've waited too long to play the mating game, as you call it, but I just can't keep up with her. I've always felt a guy should be able to count on the woman he's involved with!"

"Are you telling me you're actually involved with Lili?"

Tom ran a finger around the rim of his glass. "You might say so."

Lucas reached for the glass of ale the waiter set on the scarred oak table in front of him, and took a deep swallow. "Don't tell me, let me guess," he said as he popped a pretzel into his mouth. "This is where I'm supposed to come in, right?"

Tom grinned ruefully. "You bet. I figure that any man who was able to tame a strong-minded individual like April has to have some clues on how to handle a woman."

"I'm a sociologist, Tom," Lucas answered with a shrug and a sympathetic smile. "When it comes to understanding a woman, what you need is a miracle. If you can't find one, then find a psychologist. Preferably someone who claims to know what makes a woman tick. As for me, I haven't a clue."

"Come on. You tamed April, didn't you?"

Lucas burst into laughter. "What you don't seem to realize is that April tamed me!"

"That's a load of bull!" Tom said in disbelief. He'd worked with April long enough to know she was an independent and creative woman, but to have the upper hand with Sullivan? No way! "What about those six rules of yours? Don't tell me they didn't work on April?"

"Nope," Lucas confessed with a satisfied grin. "By the time April got through showing me what real women are like and rubbing my nose in those misguided rules, I was putty in her hands."

"You're putting me on."

"Nope. And furthermore, let me tell you, I've decided I'd much rather have a wife like April than someone who fits those damn rules of mine. Hell, I'd be bored out of my skull with what's being called a 'Sullivan woman,' and so would you."

"So, you don't have any advice to pass on about how to manage a woman like Lili?" Tom asked morosely.

Lucas laughed. "I guess all you have to do is remember the chemistry between you or whatever attracted you to Lili in the first place. I take it you *do* recall a few good things about her, right?"

Tom thought about Lili's intelligent, radiant smile. Her genuine and enthusiastic interest in his artistic alter ego. She made the creative side of him seem important, when everyone else had dismissed his interest in art as a hobby.

Then, too, there was the sexy side of her and the way she whispered erotic messages in French to him while they were making love. Universal messages he didn't need a translation for.

Lili might not exactly be the woman Lucas had described in his study, but for a while she'd come damn close. The problem now was that Tom wasn't sure which woman Lili was today.

As for the other problems he had with her, maybe a man had to take the good with the bad.

Lucas munched pretzels and smiled at the expression on Tom's face. "I take it you do remember?"

He nodded, but he wasn't about to answer. There was no way he intended to share such intimate thoughts with anyone but Lili.

"There are a few things that attracted me to Lili," he finally agreed, "but fat lot of good that's going to do me. Not as long as she keeps coming up with those wild ideas of hers. Unfortunately, it doesn't look as if she's going to stop. So, what am I supposed to do now? Continue to find a way to help to keep her out of trouble, or let her go ahead with the damn contest until she finally makes the building's management tell me to fire her?"

Lucas nodded solemnly. "I'm not sure this is what you want to hear, but since Lili's a friend of April's, and I understand they're a lot alike, I don't think you have a chance of changing her."

"Tell me about it! So, what's the bottom line?" Tom felt as much in the dark about how to handle a woman now as he had thirty minutes ago.

"The bottom line, as I see it, is that if you still feel

the chemistry that brought the two of you together, then keep an eye on her and wait her out."

Tom stared into his empty glass as if it was a fortune teller's crystal ball, but all he saw was glass, beer foam and trouble.

He didn't intend to sit around and wait to find out what was coming next. Resolving his personal relationship with Lili would have to be put on hold.

One way or another, he had to do something to save her from herself.

Chapter Thirteen

Time for the lion's den! Lili thought with a gulp.

After a hurried series of clandestine meetings with representatives from each floor in the Riverview, she was ready. Not that she was looking forward to the visit, but it was time to obtain management's permission for the contest or take Tom's advice and leave fund-raising to him.

She couldn't back off now, she told herself righteously. Quitting wasn't in her nature. She was going to launch the contest no matter what Tom might think of her.

With an emergency meeting for management and the building's owner only a week away, there was no use in trying to delay the inevitable. It was, as she saw it, simply a question of appealing to Kagan's better nature, if he had one, and to get him to listen to reason.

"Lili? Lili?" An unfamiliar male voice startled her out of her reverie. She hurriedly swung around to meet Homer Eldridge's inquiring gaze.

"I guess you didn't hear me the first time I called out to you," the senior Eldridge said. When Lili started to apologize, he interrupted, "I think I have a pretty good idea of what's troubling you."

Tom's father wore a suit of brown and beige and a white polo shirt that matched his wavy hair. The twinkle in his blue eyes and his broad smile reminded her of Tom. If she hadn't felt guilty about the contest notes spread on her desk, she would have been pleased to see him. How could she not like a man who, according to Tom, was so taken with her children that he hoped to become their grandfather?

Lili slid off her stool and held out her hand in welcome. "I'm sorry I didn't hear you call, Mr. Eldridge. You are right. I was thinking about a small problem I have."

"A small problem?" Homer's eyebrows rose in wry amusement as he took Lili's hand in his. "To be honest, Tom's already told me about this problem of yours—a contest to raise money, if I remember. Come, my dear, why don't we sit down, and you can tell me all about it."

Lili remembered the senior Eldridge's strong reaction to the plane and banner at the magazine's picnic. The last thing she wanted now was to say anything that might give him a heart attack. "Thank you," she said with a grateful smile, "but it must be a secret for now."

"Even if I tell you I'm here because I would like to be of some help with this problem of yours?"

Lili's fears of giving away her plans almost melted at the look of genuine interest in the older man's eyes.

"I am afraid it is about Mr. Kagan and his plans to close the center," she explained. "If you weren't able to persuade him to listen to you before, I don't know how you will be able to convince him to listen now."

"That was before, Lili, and this is now." Homer patted her hand in a fatherly manner that touched her heart.

No matter what Tom said about his father being uninterested in children during Tom's youth, he appeared to have changed. He was a family man now.

Homer motioned Lili to a seat and sat down beside her. "I've known Jules Kagan for a long time. Now that he's had a chance to cool off, I think I just might get through to him. He's not all bad, Lili. After all, he helped start the center."

Lili smiled wistfully. "My grandmother used to say 'from your lips to God's ear,' at troublesome times, but I don't know if even God could change Mr. Kagan's mind."

"I think I'll be able to resolve this little problem of yours sooner than you think. Although it never hurts to add a small prayer when something is important to you," he answered wryly. "That's one reason why I'm here, my dear. You may remember I told you I was one of the founders of the child care operation when Kagan bought the building?"

"Yes." Lili sensed that while Tom's father's sponsorship of the center was reason enough for him to be concerned with its future, the look in his eyes told her that wasn't his only concern. "And the other reason?"

Homer sobered. "Maybe to make up for the past," he said softly. "I'm afraid I was always too busy to be a real father to Tom and Megan when they were young. I left their upbringing to their mother, a truth I regret to this day. Don't get me wrong. Tom has never complained, but I know my absence must have affected him deeply."

He paused a moment, but when he spoke again, his voice grew strong and determined. "Are you and Tom engaged?"

Lili hesitated. How could she answer the question when she wasn't sure herself? "I think so," she answered, "but I am not certain."

"If so, my dear, I hope to be a better grandfather to your twins and to any future children you and Tom may have than I was a father to my own children."

With hope in her heart, Lili began to understand Tom's reluctance to make commitments where children were concerned. Without a role model of his own, he must be afraid he would not be a better father to his own children than his father had been to him. More importantly, she began to understand Tom's reluctance to be around her twins.

"Have you told this to Tom?"

"No," Homer said with a helpless shrug. "It's hard to say some things to a grown man. At this point in time, I'm not even sure if it would change our relationship if I did. I'm certain he only remembers me as a father who was hardly ever there for him and," he added ruefully, "an appendage to a magazine I considered more important than him."

At the older man's remorse, Lili murmured in sympathy. She sensed there was no way he would have bared his soul if he hadn't cared for her and truly believed she and Tom were engaged to be married. Or, perhaps more importantly, if he hadn't thought he would someday become a grandfather to her children.

If her engagement to Tom was something more than a convenience to be broken at his will, she would have felt honored at Homer's trust in her. Instead, she felt guilty at being party to a lie.

"I'm not anxious to see the center close any more than you are, my dear," he stated when she was silent.

"So go ahead. Tell me what's on your mind and leave Jules Kagan to me. I promise you he'll listen to me this time. Even if I have to tackle and hog-tie him while I talk some sense into him."

Grateful at the change of topic, Lili went on to explain the contest. And when Homer nodded in approval, she told him that the idea had been enthusiastically received by the employees in the building.

"I must start the contest right away, and certainly before Mr. Kagan's meeting with the tenants," Lili added worriedly. "I made an appointment to speak to his manager this afternoon, to get his permission to go ahead."

Homer looked doubtful. "And you expect to accomplish all of this and the contest in one week's time?"

"Perhaps not all," Lili admitted, her fears growing by the minute as she realized how little time was left. "At least we can show Mr. Kagan we are all willing to do our share to keep the center open."

"Time, Lili." Homer patted her hand. "You need time, and I'm afraid you don't have much of it left. It's not only Jules's blessings to go ahead with the contest that you need, it will take time for all those events to take place."

He broke into a broad grin. "That bachelor and bachelorette auction idea of yours—it's one of the best schemes to raise money that I've heard of in a long time!"

Lili shuddered as she recalled Tom's reaction to her plans. "I'm afraid Tom doesn't think so."

Homer grinned. "Perhaps, but don't let that stop you." The twinkle in his eyes took years off his age. "Of course, it depends on whom you decide to auction. If you're interested, I might have someone in mind."

Lili was afraid to ask who the person might be. "You are sure about this?"

"Trust me, everything will work out fine," he assured her. "That is, if you can bring yourself to ignore my son and go through with your plans?"

Lili recalled Tom's reaction to the contest and the auction. Thank goodness he didn't know he was Rita's choice as the bachelor.

"No," she said, with a silent prayer that Rita had forgotten the idea of using Tom in the auction. "I am not sure if involving you is a good idea. I would not want to cause trouble between you and Tom."

Lili would have felt a lot better if she had squelched Rita's plans. "If we decide to go through with the auction, I'm not sure who the man will be," Lili told him. "I have asked that it not be Tom. I think your son is old-fashioned enough to believe that bake sales and rummage sales are the only things women are good at. I'm not sure he knows that women today are looking for more exciting things to do, just as men are."

Tom's father chuckled in sympathy. "That sounds like my son. Still, I have a feeling you're just the woman to show him the truth."

Lili wasn't sure anymore.

When she said nothing, Homer smiled and patted her knee. "So, back to the contest. How much time do you think you'll need?"

"At least one week to get ready and two more for all the events?"

"How about I negotiate with Kagan? I'll see if I can get you a month."

Before Lili could answer, Tom strode into the studio and approached his father. "What in the hell is going on here?"

When Lili gasped at Tom's language, Homer shot her

a perceptive look before he answered casually, "Just visiting. Why?"

"Because you haven't shown up in the office for a long time." Tom glanced at Lili suspiciously. "Why here and why now? For that matter, what plot are you and Lili hatching?"

His father shrugged. "I may have retired as the magazine's publisher, but don't forget that I still own *Today's World,* Son. There's no reason why I can't drop into the studio now and then to visit."

"You told me you were going fishing!"

"One man's idea of fishing isn't the same as another's," his father said placidly. "Besides, there's no law that says a man can't change his mind. As for my being here with Lili, we were just getting acquainted. Since I understand she's going to be my daughter-in-law one of these days, I thought it would be good to get to know her better." When Tom was silent, his father added, "You are engaged to Lili, aren't you?"

Tom eyed Lili warily. "You might say so."

"Then I will," his father said firmly. "And if there's any question about it, I suggest you and Lili get together and make up your minds."

To add to Lili's growing unease, Tom eyed her dubiously. "I don't know about you, Dad, but personally, I never know what Lili's up to from one day to the next. When you figure her out, let me in on the secret."

"No problem," his father answered, with a reassuring wink at her. "Marriage to Lili will keep you on your toes. By the way, my dear, when's the happy wedding date? Soon, I hope?"

Lili's eyes widened as she looked at Tom, silently asking him to help explain an engagement that to her was still unexplainable. Especially since, from the look on his face, it was beginning to seem as if their engagement of convenience was no longer convenient. "I am not sure. Tom?"

His lips tightened. "I'm afraid that depends."

Homer thoughtfully rubbed his chin. "Oh? On what?"

"On just what kind of game Lili's been playing."

Shocked, she stared at Tom. It took only a moment to realize he actually believed she'd been playing a game with him from the beginning. It even sounded as if he believed she'd been trying to fool him when she'd agreed to his offer of a convenient engagement. Was it possible that he thought her agreement would allow her to continue activities that he felt jeopardized not only his business lease with Kagan, but perhaps even his magazine's future?

Lili's heart grew heavy. Instead of the man with whom she'd hoped to share the future, Tom had become someone she scarcely knew.

Like his father, he was a man for whom *Today's World* magazine came first.

Had his whispers and promises been only to buy her silence?

Lili lifted her chin proudly. "There was no game before this moment and there is no game now. Whatever you think I have done is only what a woman must do for the good of many children, not just her own."

"And, as usual, that woman has to be you," Tom said dispiritedly. "As for you, Dad, my advice is not to let yourself get involved in this mess. Someone, and you know I mean Lili, is going to be hurt if this keeps on."

"Come now, Son," Homer chided. "Since Lili and I

were only visiting, aren't you being a little hard on her?"

Tom avoided Lili's eyes. "No. Take it from me, I know I'm right. It isn't as if I don't understand what Lili was trying to do. Hell, I even promised to help raise the funds she needs if she would only back off and give me some space. I guess I was asking for the impossible."

Through tear-filled eyes, Lili watched as Tom shot her a cool look and strode out of the studio, taking the last of her hopes and dreams with him.

Homer put his arm around her shoulders. "I'm not sure just what that was all about, my dear, but you have my word that everything is going to turn out okay. Tom may be angry at the moment, but I'm still willing to help you. And not only for the children, but for you. As for my son, whatever is eating him right now, I'm sure that in time it can be straightened out. Give him a chance to cool off, then make him talk things over with you."

Lili dried her eyes. Only once before in her life, when her husband had been taken from her, had she ever felt such a hollow, lonely feeling. Today, her second chance at happiness had flown. "It is more than that. Contest aside, I am afraid I have lost Tom's trust. Without trust, how can there be a future for us?"

"We'll see," Homer said quietly, handing her a large white handkerchief he pulled out of his pocket. "Here, dry those tears, and remember that whatever has happened here hasn't changed my mind. I'm going to keep positive thoughts about you becoming my daughter-in-law, and I suggest you do the same. As for Jules, I intend to speak to him on your behalf. Now, wipe your eyes and get ready for your meeting. There's nothing better than a positive attitude to get what you want. I'll be back in touch with you soon."

Lili smiled through her tears. She didn't know how Tom's father intended to get Kagan to change his mind, but at the moment the senior Eldridge had become her knight in shining armor. And not just for offering to help her in her fight to save the day care. No matter what Tom thought about him, his father was a kindly and good man. "You would do this for me, Mr. Eldridge?"

"For all of us, my dear," Homer replied with a look that warmed her heart. "My son included. By the way," he continued as he turned to go, "I hope you'll be calling me Dad one day very soon."

Wistfully, Lili watched him leave. She cherished his assumption that she would become part of his family, even as she doubted that the time would ever come.

By TWO-THIRTY, Lili was reduced to chewing the ends of her pencil. Finding April or Rita and pouring out her heart would be too hurtful. Involving anyone else in her problem was out of the question. If anyone was going to get fired over the contest, it would have to be her.

She went back to trying to work on her new assignment, a background for a travel article on cruising with small children. Ideas, once so readily available, became a jumble in her mind. All she could think of was Homer Eldridge's confrontation with Jules Kagan and her own meeting with management.

To her surprise, Tom came back into the studio carrying a folder under his arm. "Okay," he said as if he hadn't stormed out of the studio a short time ago, "if I can't persuade you to listen to reason and to forget the contest, let's look at it as a business proposition. How much money do you think you'll need to keep the center open for now?"

"Six thousand a month?"

Tom frowned. "You don't sound too sure about that."

Lili straightened up. She was no businesswoman, but she had nothing to lose by asking for the moon. "Maybe a little more."

"Okay. We'll go for seven thousand." He flipped open a spreadsheet and made a few entries. "Go ahead and tell me the probable events for the fund-raiser."

Questioning her sanity, Lili pulled out the list. "Portraits, a rummage sale, a block party, a—"

"Hold it right there!" Tom commanded. "I need to know the expected costs for each of these events versus possible return. Otherwise this is a futile exercise."

"There are no costs," Lili answered proudly. "Since everything is being donated, the money raised will be all profit!"

"You hope. Go ahead. Start again."

"The bake sale is to come first."

"Fine," Tom agreed. "I take it the ingredients are donated. Now, how much do you intend to pay the judges?"

"Since Theo Mecouri, in the interest of fairness, has obtained the services of a well-known chef who's a friend of his, there is no cost for a judge. You might also be interested to know that there has been a great stir of excitement among the contestants. Some of them want to become chefs."

"Great," Tom muttered. "How many entrants have signed up?"

"So far, sixteen. With the contestants' baking for sale at the end of the contest, I expect a respectable return for the event."

"Next?"

"The rummage and flea market sales. White elephant and other donations are already accumulating in a storage room in the parking area. As for financial returns, I don't know what they might be."

"Next?"

"There is the lemonade stand proposed by the proprietor of the coffee kiosk in the lobby. The most we can hope to make is a few hundred dollars, but every little bit helps."

Tom frowned as he wrote down another figure. "Go on."

"Hansen's Elite Photography, the third-floor entry, is offering portraits at a reduced price of fifty dollars each, so they have a good chance at winning the contest."

"Maybe," Tom replied with a scowl. "That still isn't going to be enough."

Lili glanced at her list. She hated to admit Tom was right, but she wasn't ready to give up.

"The most lucrative means of raising funds is probably going to be the block party at the end. But we must find a place to hold it," she added thoughtfully. "Maybe, if the weather holds, at Navy Pier? Someone suggested that. If not, there are indoor places to hold the event."

Tom nodded. "At least that's a good idea. But only if the party's open to the public. You *could,* if you explained the reason for the event, ask Navy Pier's management for a more generous percentage of the take for the day."

Lili felt herself blanch at the thought of approaching the facility. Taking her plan to Riverview's management was daunting enough.

"Okay," Tom said as he closed the folder. "I guess that still leaves me with a job to do. I'll talk to you later."

With that, he strode out of the studio.

A glance at her watch told Lili that her fund-raising volunteers, Sandra Selby and Horace Atkins, who both had small children in day care, were late again. Enthusiasm at the meeting in the cafeteria had evidently been one thing. A face-to-face with the building's management was another.

Not that she blamed them, she thought as she aimlessly sketched a poolside scene with children in swimsuits aboard a cruise ship. Good jobs were hard to find.

The alarm on her watch finally signaled three-thirty, time for her appointment upstairs. Murmuring a silent prayer for both herself and Tom, she gathered her notes and headed for the door.

"SOUNDS HARMLESS," Bill Ashford, the manager of the Riverview, said when Lili explained her plans. "What does Tom Eldridge think of this? After all, you do work for him."

Lili swallowed the lump in her throat and tried to find a middle ground between the truth and a white lie. "Tom knows about the contest. Of course," she added with a smile, "I didn't have the entire list of proposed events to show him at the time."

The man's eyes lit up as he peered at her over his glasses. "A contest sounds a lot less harmful than those damn fliers and petitions we've been seeing around here recently. I'll talk to Mr. Kagan and see what he thinks about this. In the meantime," he murmured, "do you have plans for dinner tonight?"

Lili stared at Ashford. She'd hoped to encourage him

to help her, but it looked as if she'd gone too far. The last thing she needed was to incur Tom's wrath by having him hear she'd accepted a dinner invitation with this man. It would only reinforce Tom's opinion that she used her femininity to her advantage. She decided to play dumb. "Dinner?"

"Yeah," Bill answered with a grin. "I've noticed you around the building before, and to tell you the truth, I liked what I saw. I just wasn't sure you were available. How about it?"

Lili smiled. "I am very busy with the contest for the next week." She stood to leave. "Perhaps another time. In the meanwhile, I would appreciate hearing from you about this. Maybe by tomorrow?"

Hardly put off, Bill glanced at the list Lili had slid across the table for Kagan's approval. "Maybe. Of course..." he eyed Lili in a way that made her uneasy "...we'd have to make sure the owner doesn't have any liability in all of this before I get him to agree to it. I'll let you know in a day or two."

"I don't have a day or two," Lili protested. "The contest must be under way by the time of Mr. Kagan's meeting!"

Ashford shrugged as if the delay was no problem, but she sensed he wasn't pleased with her. "I'm afraid Kagan will say it's a question of rising costs and not enough money to spread around. At any rate, you think about a dinner date and I'll think about trying to persuade Kagan. Okay?"

With a quick nod, Lili smiled and backed out of his office before he could insist on an answer. Dating anyone, let alone a man who was so obviously trying to coerce her, was out of the question. Even though, according to Rita, Lili was resorting to blackmail herself, her heart belonged to Tom. The only thing was, she could no longer be sure he wanted it.

On her way back to the studio, all she could think of was what it must have cost Tom to keep silent when he'd found out she was the one stirring up the building's occupants. Was it a sign he really cared about her?

Had Tom's anger been an excuse not to tell her how he felt about her? *If* he cared about her at all?

Perhaps she'd misjudged him just as badly as he'd misjudged her. Maybe she should take a lesson from her friend April and try to start over. She had to show Tom how to believe in what his heart was telling him.

Even if his mind was afraid to trust her.

She'd promised to be honest with him, and the truth was that she hadn't been—-not really.

Tom had been more than her second chance at love, she mused wistfully. He'd been her chance for happiness. A life with more babies and an extended family.

Her thoughts turned to a future without Tom. The possibility that she'd lost him because of a cause someone else could have managed as well was more than she could bear.

She understood now that he was the most important person in her world.

But was it too late to do anything about it?

Chapter Fourteen

Lili was at it again!

Tom stared in disbelief at the notice posted in the elevator. After having convinced himself she was ready to listen to reason, the announcement that the building-wide contest was still on took him by surprise.

Sure, he'd discussed the proposal with her, but he hadn't actually endorsed it.

To add to his dismay, a note at the bottom of the poster, clearly in Lili's handwriting, reminded contestants to take their entries for the baking contest to the penthouse restaurant early Monday morning for judging.

Why had she gone ahead with this when he'd advised her against it? A contest wouldn't bring in enough funds to make a difference, and it might antagonize Riverview's management even more.

Hadn't he shown Lili, event by event, that she couldn't raise enough money this way?

What hadn't she understood about his assurance that *he* would try to find a major backer as long as she backed off?

Was it because he'd lost his cool when he'd found

Lili and his father deep in conversation, knowing the only topic they had in common was the child care center?

He'd apologized for losing his temper, hadn't he? Not once, but twice?

After swallowing his pride, hadn't he gone to the building's management office to sound out Bill Ashford about the possibility of a heart-to-heart meeting with Kagan, only to find Lili had beaten him to it?

What really rocked him was the way Ashford had been standing in the doorway, gazing after a departing Lili with undisguised interest in his eyes.

Unfortunately, the scene had also served to remind Tom of the tenants' penthouse party, where Lili had been surrounded by a trio of admiring men.

Tom tried to fight back his frustration. No matter how he looked at it, it was clear that she had been using her feminine wiles all along to persuade men to do what she wanted.

Including him.

He should have known better than to believe those innocent sapphire eyes.

As the elevator reached his floor, the list of entries on the poster finally registered: Lili's contest was under way and there was no turning back.

Enough was enough!

Cursing under his breath, Tom punched the button again, sending the elevator down one more floor to the magazine's art studio. This time, he wouldn't settle for just talking. This time, he intended to make it damn clear to Lili that she was to run the contest through him so he could at least monitor her activities. There was no other way to keep her out of trouble.

No sooner had he exited the elevator and headed for the art studio than Arthur, the office gofer, appeared around the corner and called to him.

Frustrated, Tom reluctantly ground to a stop. "What's up, Art? I'm in a hurry."

"Sorry, Mr. Eldridge, I just wanted to ask you if the rumor I heard about you is true."

The hair on the back of Tom's neck started to tingle—a condition he'd suffered ever since he'd gotten involved with Lili. "What about me?"

"The bachelor auction." Arthur grinned sheepishly. "Alice is a romantic woman. She wouldn't forgive me if I didn't find out if the rumor is true. You know how women are."

Tom glanced at the door to the art studio. "Yeah, unfortunately I do know. Who's Alice and what's this about an auction?"

"Alice is my fiancée," Arthur answered shyly. "We're getting married in a few weeks."

Tom remembered. There'd been a veritable rash of employee weddings in the last two months, reminding everyone that it was spring, and time for the mating game. "And?"

"Like I said, Alice is an incurable romantic. I can't wait to tell her if the rumor's true. Is it?"

Tom's mind was on confronting Lili, but Arthur's remark about the auction finally registered. "And what does the rumor have to do with me?"

Arthur shook his head. "I've got to hand it to you, Mr. Eldridge. Auctioning you off for a dinner date is real cool. I heard the single women in the building are checking their bank balances. You *are* going to be the lucky guy, right?"

Tom's blood ran cold. An auction was bad enough, but with him as the prize?

He'd already learned that Lili was a strong and determined woman, but this was going too far! His warning might have been ignored, but he would never have suspected she'd have the nerve to use him as the prize. Hell! Not when she knew how he felt about keeping a low profile with his employees. And certainly not after their own romantic interlude.

Or had that night been just another way for Lili to snare him?

"Don't believe everything you hear, Art," he said as he turned away. "Someone's just trying to have some fun at my expense."

No wonder Lili had gone along with his offer of an engagement of convenience, Tom thought as he strode toward the studio. The agreement had given her time to put her plans into action.

If she'd thought she was following one of Lucas Sullivan's rules, trying to make Tom feel masculine by volunteering him as the contest prize, she was way off the mark.

According to Sullivan, Lili should have reined in her own desires to promote the health of their relationship.

The actual truth was that if she'd really cared about him, she would have known he preferred a supportive Sullivan-type woman instead of a woman with a misguided sense of independence.

It wasn't as if he'd asked a lot of Lili, he told himself. All he'd expected was that she be reasonable and leave the center's survival to him.

He stopped just outside the studio door. Considering the mood he was in, maybe it would be better to put off confronting Lili until he'd had a chance to cool down.

Tom glanced at his watch. He'd almost forgotten he'd promised Mrs. London he'd work with little Tommy, the artist, for an hour or two today.

Surely the reminder was an omen, he decided as he turned back to the elevators. And would provide him with a break from his problems with Lili.

"AH! MR. ELDRIDGE. At last!" Mary London beamed at Tom when she answered his knock on the secured door. "You've come just at the right time," she whispered. "Tommy has finally finished the painting of what he calls his pumpkin orchard. In fact, he told me he's drawn the painting just for you. Imagine that." She turned and led the way into the room where the children were playing. "You must have made quite an impression on that first visit," she added with an admiring glance back at Tom.

Ashamed of the time that had passed since his promise to return to the day care, Tom felt guilty as hell. He'd been so wrapped up with Lili that he'd forgotten he might be able to make a positive contribution by working with a little boy, instead of spending all his time trying to keep Lili out of trouble. A futile expectation if there ever was one, he thought.

"I think Tommy was just happy that someone took an interest in his work," Tom whispered as he followed Mrs. London into the main room, where small children were sitting on a rug and listening to a story.

"You underestimate yourself," Mrs. London whispered. "You do know that your father was one of our founders, don't you?"

Tom nodded.

"You're an admirable son of a wonderful man, and don't you forget it. Of course," she added with a rueful smile, "your father didn't go quite so far as you seem to have."

Speechless, Tom could only nod again.

"Oh, and by the way, " Mrs. London called after him. "I did want to say that it's good of you to allow yourself to be auctioned off on our behalf. You've certainly impressed me," she added with a teasing smile, "but unfortunately, I don't think I can afford you."

Afford him! First Arthur and now Mrs. London. How many others knew of his role in the auction—one that, if asked, he would never have considered? No wonder people had been grinning at him all day.

He headed to the corner where Tommy was setting up a fresh sheet of drawing paper. As soon as his time with the kid was over, he was going to find Lili and see to it she spread the word he wasn't going to be the sucker auctioned off.

He rolled up his sleeves and called to Tommy. The little boy would distract him, he thought as the child broke into a smile. At least Tommy was too young and too innocent to understand the ridiculous rumor floating around the building, even if he'd heard it.

As for Tommy's passion for pumpkins, all Tom had to do was convince him that pumpkins grew on vines, not on trees.

Or maybe it might be wise to leave well enough alone. Maybe, in Tommy's safe little world, pumpkins *did* grow on trees. As for Tom, he had to live in the real world.

LILI STARED AT ARTHUR when he stopped to offer her a cup of coffee. "What did you say?"

Arthur's grin faded at Lili's reaction to his harmless question. "I said I thought Mr. Eldridge would be the last person who would agree to be auctioned off as our entry in the contest."

Lili's eyes widened. This must be Rita's doing. Using Tom hadn't been her idea. Having a man stand on a stage while women bid for him was bad enough. What would Tom say when he found Rita had spread the rumor that he had agreed to be auctioned off, gambling that he would be too proud to deny it?

Lili wouldn't blame him for believing she'd planned to use their relationship against him, and had ignored his warning.

"Gee, Lili," Arthur said, "I'm really sorry. I thought you knew all about the rumor that Mr. Eldridge is the bachelor being auctioned, or I wouldn't have joked about it."

She shuddered. "It's not your fault, Arthur. I have to find him and explain it was all a mistake! When did you last see him?"

"Punching the down button on the elevator," Arthur said as he began to push the refreshment cart down the hall. "He didn't tell me where he was going, but he sure looked mad."

Lili waved goodbye. If Tom had taken the down elevator, the most likely place he could be headed for was the day care center, or, heaven forbid, the cafeteria in the basement, where detailed information regarding the contest was posted on the community bulletin board.

She reached for her cell phone and called the number Homer had given her. If anyone could help her deflect Tom's anger, it was his father. When no one answered, she left an SOS message and headed for Rita's office.

"Rita, we have to talk!"

When her friend murmured something under her breath but didn't look up from her computer, Lili reached over her shoulder and turned off the monitor.

"Great," Rita grumbled. "I was in the middle of some critical research."

"Maybe so," Lili retorted. Now that she had her attention, she rushed on. "I am in the middle of a bigger crisis, and all because of you. How could you spread a rumor that Tom had volunteered to be auctioned off for the contest? You had to know he would be against the idea."

Unrepentant, Rita turned her monitor back on and grinned. "Because it was the only way I knew to get him to cooperate, that's why. From what I hear around the building, everyone believes he's going to do it. Tom will have to go along."

"That is what I am afraid of!"

"Yeah, Tom can't back out now even if he wanted to. We're going to rake in a bundle, and our floor is going to win the contest. New York City, here I come!"

Lili dropped into a chair and ran her fingers over her aching forehead. "I do not believe this!"

"Wait until I tell you I've also decided to auction off a woman," Rita added. "Of course, her identity is going to be a secret until the day of the auction. I can give you a hint, if you like."

"I do not like," Lili moaned, at Rita's lack of remorse. "If Tom should ask me, I would rather not know. I have enough to worry about."

"It's a little late to worry, kiddo, but think of all the money auctioning a man off as a dinner date will bring in. In fact," Rita added, "I have another idea that's even better than that."

Lili's head began to pound. "I have heard enough." She tried to tell herself Rita meant well. That surely Tom would realize his being auctioned off was only for a dinner date. She shook her head. Who was she kidding?

She knew there was a bigger problem between herself and Tom than the contest. He was a take-charge man and, despite her serene outward manner, she was an extremely independent woman. "I have to find Tom!"

"No, Lili, wait a minute!" Rita bounced to her feet. "If you don't like the idea of an auction, I have a better idea. If you think Tom would be embarrassed, how about we switch the auction to a raffle? We could charge ten dollars a ticket and make a bundle."

Lili had started to feel relieved, until she heard Rita's new idea.

"We can still use Tom as the prize."

"You can't just *sell* Tom this way," she groaned. "Auctioning him off as a dinner date is a bad idea, but a raffle isn't much better. You cannot do this."

"Maybe not," Rita said with a wicked grin, "but not all the women in the building would agree with you. Most of them would love to go out to dinner with him whether they're willing to admit it or not. April and I might not believe he's a hottie, but you're not the only woman who thinks he is. The fact that he's also rich and single can't hurt."

Lili despaired over Rita's lack of remorse. Tom might

be considered a "hottie," but until this morning, he'd been *her* hottie—if only for pretend. "Rita, how *could* you?"

"Come on, Lili," her friend teased. "This isn't just about you and Tom anymore. It's about keeping the center open."

Lili slid to the edge of her chair and eyed Rita with growing suspicion. She was up to something—something more than just raffling off Tom. Lili could feel it in her bones. "You talk as if you have already made up your mind about this change."

"I'm afraid so," Rita agreed. "To be honest, I've just come back from the cafeteria. I switched our floor's contest entry from an auction to a raffle. In fact, I'm having tickets run off in our print shop even as we speak. I tell you, we're going to make a bundle."

Lili gasped. "No!"

"Yes," Rita replied airily. "I intend to change the notice in the elevators before I go home tonight."

Lili shot out of her chair and with a muttered "*merde*" made for the door.

"Hey, wait a minute," Rita called. "Where are you going?"

"To keep the sky from falling before it is too late," Lili called over her shoulder.

WHEN LILI BARRELED into the cafeteria, Tom was already staring at the bulletin board.

Breathless, she skidded to a stop beside him. "Before you say anything, I swear I did not do this. You must believe me."

To her dismay, he looked at her as if she were a stranger instead of the woman he'd made love to such a short time ago. "Oh, I believe you all right," he said dryly. "You might have been creating incendiary fliers, circulating petitions and charming men to get your way, but not even you would dream up a caper like this one. From the way the notice reads, I seem to be the prize."

Lili let out a sigh of relief. "Then you are not angry with me?"

"Angry?" Tom turned away with an unconvincing shrug. "No, Lili. I'm beyond anger. I trusted you before, but no more. Whoever is behind this raffle idea is going to look like a fool when she can't produce the raffle prize." He gestured to the bulletin board.

"She?" Lili's antennae quivered. If Tom wasn't accusing her of being the mastermind behind the raffle, he had to have some idea who the culprit was.

He eyed her in a detached way that frightened her more than if he'd actually lost his temper. "I assume it's one of your friends trying to help you? Too bad I'm not playing."

Lili's joy in the fund-raising turned to dust. "This is something bigger than both of us, Tom. You know the contest is important. I beg you to reconsider. Not for me, but for all the children."

When Tom looked at her, Lili realized she'd struck a sympathetic note.

"You might be right," he answered. "Now that you and your friends have gotten this far, I suppose there are too many people involved for me to back out of the stunt."

"And this engagement of convenience of ours?" Lili asked.

"Over," he answered in a defeated tone. "It's finally gotten through to me that the idea was a stupid one to begin with. I've never been able to influence my father, and it looks as if I can't change your mind, either. You're determined to go your own way no matter what I say." He paused and gazed at Lili. "Tell me something. Why did you agree to the idea in the first place? I've never been sure."

"Because I believed in you," Lili whispered. "I hoped you believed in me."

"Really?" He gestured to the bulletin board. "The last thing this looks like is that you believed in me. I'm sorry, Lili, but I don't think we can work together comfortably, not anymore. I hate to say it, but I've had enough of trying to convince you to back off. Go ahead with your contest. After that, whatever happens is up to you."

Noting Tom's dejected body language as he left for the elevator, Lili realized how much she'd lost.

The telephone rang. "Lili, it's for you!" the cafeteria manager called.

Distracted by her anguish, Lili reached for the phone. By the time she'd listened to the caller, agreed to a meeting and hung up, she was in a daze.

Had the message come too late?

Chapter Fifteen

First thing Monday morning, Rita stormed into Tom's office. "You can't do this to Lili!"

Tom raised an eyebrow. "I can't?"

"No, you can't!" she answered. "I've just come from the art studio. Lili told me you've broken up with her. Come on, Tom, you know she means a lot to all of us. I can't see her so unhappy over something I caused."

Tom got up, closed the office door and strode back to his desk. "I was under the impression I'm a grown man. And since I am, it seems to me I can do anything I have to do."

Rita crossed her arms and, instead of being intimidated, stood her ground. "You don't *have* to do this," she retorted. "Lili doesn't deserve this kind of treatment."

Tom eyed Rita meaningfully. "Considering I think—no, scratch that," he said, as he sat down behind his desk. "Considering that I *know* it was you and Lili together behind the raffle idea, you're damn lucky I didn't fire her. You, on the other hand, are something else."

Rita sniffed scornfully. "I'm not sure why you're so set on blaming Lili, but we're good friends and I can't let you treat her like this. Since I believe you really do care for her, I would have thought you'd be grateful I'm sticking up for her."

"Grateful for making me look like a fool?" Tom answered bitterly. "That's a laugh." He wasn't prepared to tell Rita that the last thing he'd wanted was to break off with Lili.

He felt a twinge of shame. He'd engineered the pretend engagement to keep his dad from nagging him about marriage. Who would have thought that Lili would change his mind and make him want the real thing?

Without realizing what had happened, he'd fallen in love with her, starting the day he'd gone looking for the culprit who was stirring up the building's occupants. Considering he'd caught Lili in the act of making another flier, he should have fired her on the spot. Instead, he'd fallen for sapphire eyes, a sweet smile and, heaven help him, her charming accent.

And yet…how could he love a woman who didn't trust him to keep his word? A woman who hadn't stopped championing her cause even after he'd promised to help her if she did? The cause was apparently more important to her than he was.

"Grateful?" he snorted. "My life's been in a turmoil from the moment I discovered Lili was the person behind those damn fliers. Personally, I don't have an argument with trying to save the center, even though that's not my problem. My real problem is that a clause in my lease says if I or any of my employees do anything to defame the Riverview's owner or management, the lease is canceled."

"Oh come on, Tom," Rita objected. "There's nothing about Lili's crusade that defames anyone. Certainly not the contest."

"Try telling that to the owner," Tom said sourly. "He wasn't too happy over the fliers, but that damn airplane stunt was the final straw. It really ticked him off."

Rita blushed.

"Yeah," Tom said, with a look intended to tell her she'd given herself away. "I'm pretty sure who was behind that stunt, and it wasn't Lili. Still, she's at it again with that damn raffle. How can I turn a blind eye when I never know what she's going to come up with next?"

"You can't just sit there and tell me you want Lili to become a 'Stepford wife' at your beck and call. Or a 'Sullivan woman.' Heck, from what April tells me, even Lucas doesn't believe in those rules anymore, so why would you?"

"No, I didn't want Lili to be a 'Stepford wife' or a 'Sullivan woman' before, and I don't want her to be one now!" Tom thundered. "But I sure as hell can't let her fight me all the way! That damn raffle idea with me as the prize is the final straw. If things keep going the way they have been, I might wind up not having a magazine to worry about. Hell, a man can take only so much."

He reached for the phone. "I have work to do, and so do you. If you're through defending Lili, count yourself lucky you're not joining the unemployment lines, and get back to work!"

"But—but I'm not finished," Rita stammered. "If you really care for Lili, I have another idea I'm sure you'll go for."

Tom pointed to the door. "As far as I'm concerned, we're through talking."

With a chilling glare, Rita marched to the office

doorway, then paused. "I've always thought of you as one of the good-guy bosses. I even thought you could take a joke. But I never would have thought you cared for the magazine more than you did your employees." She slammed the door behind her on her way out.

Uneasy over Rita's defense of Lili, Tom sat back with a sinking feeling. He'd been so sure he'd done the right thing by breaking off with Lili, but maybe Rita was right. Now that he thought about it, was keeping the magazine housed in the Riverview more important to him than Lili was?

He reached for the intercom and asked his secretary to call down to the art studio and ask Lili to come up.

TEN MINUTES LATER, Lili appeared. "You wished to see me?"

"Yes, I did." Tom motioned for her to come into the office and close the door behind her. "Sit down for a moment, please." The sight of Lili's clenched hands damn near broke his heart. The drawn look on her face stirred his soul. How could he have been so cruel to the woman he loved?

He was tempted to take her in his arms and apologize, but the tense look on her face warned him to keep his distance. First he'd get his apology off his chest, then he'd spend the rest of his life showing her how much he loved her.

"I haven't had a moment's peace since I lost my temper," he said, pausing at her side. "The truth is, I asked you to come here because I wanted to tell you I'm sorry for losing my temper. I realize I behaved like a stupid, unthinking jerk."

The expression on Lili's face wasn't reassuring.

"I've had a chance to think about the future and I don't like what I see," Tom said as he paced the office floor. "I've come to realize that the future of the magazine doesn't depend on our being located in the Riverview. Hell, even if Kagan breaks my lease, it doesn't matter anymore. It's not that big a deal. I can publish the magazine anywhere. I'm sure there are a number of buildings that would be happy to have us. Besides," he added with a hopeful smile, "the rent might be cheaper."

He was trying his best to make Lili grin, but it didn't seem to be working. He hated himself for what he'd done to her.

"Like I said," he mumbled, "I want to apologize for my behavior. I went overboard and I'd like to make amends."

Lili shook her head. "I am truly sorry, but working here together is no longer possible. I am thinking of accepting an offer elsewhere."

Tom pulled a startled Lili into his arms, and before she could react, kissed her with every ounce of love in him. "Leave if you have to," he whispered, "but not like this. Besides—" he kissed her again "—we *are* engaged to be married, aren't we?"

Tears came into her eyes. "Not really. The truth is that I have never understood this engagement of convenience. I've always known you never intended it to become real. But I now know for sure that your idea was only a way to keep your father happy and a way for me to stop making trouble for you."

Shaken at the tears that came into Lili's eyes, Tom wiped each one away with a gentle finger. "You can't mean that! Not after we've made such wonderful love together."

"Even then," Lili said, in a shaky voice that revealed her heartbreak. "I made a mistake in thinking you were my soul mate. I thought you felt the same way and that we belonged together. I was wrong."

"No, you were right," Tom insisted. "If you'll just give me a chance, I'll show you how much you do mean to me. Let me show you how much I love you, Lili."

She pulled out of his arms. "Without trust, there can be no love. Perhaps it would be better if I left your employment today instead of waiting until the contest is over."

Tom's heart ached, and his arms felt empty. But he'd be damned if he'd give up Lili without a fight. "Are you sure you can't find it in you to forgive me?"

"I forgive you," Lili answered slowly. "But I still believe everything has changed. It is better that I take this new job, and leave your magazine."

At her hesitation, Tom sensed Lili wasn't completely convinced she was doing the right thing by quitting. Maybe he had time. The two weeks before the contest would give him his chance to change her mind. "Okay. Providing you have permission for the contest, go ahead. All I ask is that you don't leave until the contest is over."

"Your father called and told me I have received permission from Mr. Kagan to go forward with the contest if I stop making fliers." Lili turned to leave. "If it is truly your wish, I will stay until it is over."

"It is." Tom gazed after Lili until she disappeared from sight. So far so good. He figured he might have lost the first round, but he didn't intend to lose the fight. He went back to his desk and reached for the telephone.

What he'd said to Lili had been true; he loved her—had loved her even before he'd realized he did. He was also positive Lili had loved him at one time, although he wasn't sure how she felt about him now. As far as he was concerned, they belonged together.

Furthermore, he didn't intend to sit back without making one last effort to make it up to Lili.

And although Jules Kagan didn't know it yet, Tom mused, as he waited for someone to pick up the line on the other end, the owner of the Riverview was going to do more than allow Lili to hold the contest.

Before he was through, Tom intended to convince Kagan to match the funds the contest might bring in. Once the money was combined with Tom's own contribution, plans to close the center would become a moot point—at least for now.

As for Lili, there were ways to bring her back to him.

A raffle might be a good place to start.

THE NEXT TWO WEEKS passed in a flurry of activity. The penthouse's baking contest brought in $360. Not a large amount, Lili told herself as she entered the figure in her notebook, but every little bit added up. As she'd predicted, the prized chocolate soufflé was purchased by Lucas Sullivan as a gift to his wife, April, for $100, making a total of $460.

The lobby's refreshment stand only brought in $131, but the organizers were pleased when it looked as if they were on their way to winning the booby prize.

The rummage sale brought in $578.

And Hansen's photo shop, thanks to its reputation as the best portrait studio in Chicago, generated $2,300 and was still counting. The tenants on several other floors had made a collective donation of $7,000.

Lili added up the total: $10,469.

She sighed as she realized they were still a long way from their goal. With small contributions still coming in, the only hope for raising enough money to make a difference was the raffle.

Lili studied the ticket sales for the raffle again. They were high enough to make her perk up. If Tom *was* the male raffle prize, either he was well known by the women throughout the building or there was something driving up sales that Lili wasn't aware of. She'd asked, but Rita wasn't talking.

Thoughts of Rita reminded Lili what time it was. Grabbing her purse, she headed to the cafeteria to meet her friends for lunch.

RITA'S EYES LIT UP when Lili rushed into the cafeteria. "Have I got good news for you!" she called before Lili had a chance to share her own about the money raised so far. "Someone just offered to buy a hundred raffle tickets if the woman raffled off for a date is you, Lili!"

Lili blinked. At ten dollars a ticket, that single sale alone contributed another thousand dollars to their cause. "Who would want to go out with me?" she asked.

"Come on, Rita, give!" April insisted. "What's going on here? The idea of auctioning off Tom for a dinner date is weird enough. After all, he's a magazine publisher, not a movie star or someone famous. As for selling raffle tickets on Lili, who would buy a hundred tickets?"

"Well, as I said," Rita answered with a wicked grin that made Lili's antennae quiver, "it was an *offer* to buy the tickets. The buyer said it was a go only if Lili agreed to be the woman raffled."

Raw from her confrontation with Tom, Lili said, "No. I cannot do this."

"Come on, Lili. You know it's for a good cause!"

Lili's mind almost froze at the idea of becoming a raffle prize. Still, if Tom was willing to do it, surely it couldn't be wrong. It was not knowing the name of the man who had promised to purchase the block of tickets that bothered her.

"Who would want me for a dinner date?" she asked again. "I am a single mother with two small children. What would I do with the twins?"

"In answer to your first question, I'm sure there are a lot of men who would love to go out with you," Rita said cheerfully. "As for the second, you can always hire a baby-sitter. Maybe you could even ask Tom's sister, Megan. Or for that matter, I would be happy to watch the twins."

Lili shook her head. "It is not a good idea to be friendly with Megan now. Besides, Noreen Talbot offered to be the woman you were going to auction off. Why don't you use her?"

Rita shrugged. "Noreen can do something else. The buyer wants you. All you have to say is yes, then sit back and wait. I'll make the arrangements."

"All right," Lili agreed reluctantly. The raffle was only for a dinner date, and she would never have to see the winner again. Besides, except for Tom, she had no interest in men.

"I will do this before I leave," Lili finally agreed. What she didn't say was that if Rita intended to make all the arrangements for the raffle, heaven only knew what the outcome would be.

BEFORE TOM COULD OBJECT, Rita walked into his office, planted herself in front of his desk and held up her hand for silence.

"Now, before you lose your cool again," she said. "I have just one question. Do you or do you not love Lili?"

Tom eyed her cautiously. "Why are you asking?"

Rita brushed off his answer. "How would you like to turn the idea of an engagement of convenience with Lili into a real engagement?"

"That's two questions," Tom said, throwing down his pen. "And the answer to both is that that's my business."

Rita smiled.

When it became obvious that she wasn't going to leave, Tom motioned for her to continue. The sooner she said what she had come for, the sooner he could go back to work.

"Just this. I happen to know Lili's heart is broken over her split with you. I'll even admit that what happened between the two of you is partly my fault. So, since I got her into this mess, I think it's up to me to get her out of it."

She dropped into a chair. "Now, listen up, Tom. I don't care if you are the boss. Lili might still be crazy about you, but she's received a job offer and she's going to take it. It's up to you to change her mind."

"The info that she's found a new job doesn't come as a surprise," he said. "She's already told me about it. Not that I think the decision was my finest hour," Tom admitted. "What do you suggest I do?"

· "Thought you'd never ask." Rita leaned across the desk. "Here's the deal. I've talked to Lili and she's agreed to let us raffle her off for a dinner date. That's where you come in. I'm afraid I've already put the cart before the horse by telling Lili about this, but I want you to buy a hundred raffle tickets."

"A hundred raffle tickets? What good would that do?"

"It'll give you a chance to say you're sorry."

Tom shifted uneasily in his chair. "Assuming I buy the tickets, there's no guarantee I'd be the winner."

Rita wiggled her eyebrows. "Wanna bet?"

Tom studied her for a long moment. He wouldn't put it past her to rig the raffle in his favor.

He reached into his jacket pocket for his checkbook. "How much and to whom do I write the check?"

"At ten bucks a ticket, that would make a thousand dollars," Rita answered happily. "Make it out to the Riverview Child Care Center. Since it will give you a chance to apologize to Lili, it's worth every penny."

Tom paused. "Apologize? Hell, I already tried that. The answer was no."

"Then try again." Rita handed him his pen. "Apologizing and making up can be a lot of fun."

Tom wrote the check and handed it over. "Why do I get the feeling I'm being coerced into doing something that may be a scam?"

"Because I've really gotten good at hiding the truth." Rita laughed as she accepted the check. "Besides, I learned how to bend the rules from a couple of pros."

"Yeah? Who?"

"You and Lili and that convenient engagement of yours," Rita said as she waved the check in the air. "I'll be back just as soon as I pick up the raffle tickets."

THE DAY OF THE RAFFLE draw couldn't come too soon for Riverview's office workers. The marble lobby teemed with people excitedly speculating on the identities of the two volunteers to be raffled off. It was assumed that Tom was the man, but bets were still being made as to the identity of the woman.

A stage had been constructed in the lobby, and the crowd grew quiet when Jules Kagan appeared on it.

Tom blinked. Not only had his father been able to get Kagan to agree to the contest, he'd managed to persuade the man to participate in the raffle!

Trying to fade into the woodwork, Tom stood off to one side and watched as Kagan rolled up one sleeve and prepared to select the winning raffle tickets from the drums.

The crowd fell silent, and Tom could feel the tension that pervaded the lobby.

"Okay, folks, lighten up here," Rita announced after she whistled to get everyone's attention. "The first draw is for a dinner date with the illustrious Tom Eldridge, the publisher of *Today's World*. We owe Tom a great deal for agreeing to be raffled off this way."

The crowd applauded.

"Go ahead, Mr. Kagan, pick a ticket."

Tom glanced across the sparkling glass-and-marble lobby to where Lili was standing with April and Lucas. The thought that this afternoon might be the last time he saw Lili damn near broke his heart.

If they hadn't been in such a public place, he would have marched over to her and demanded she give him another chance.

Kagan rummaged in the drum marked HIS, drew a ticket out and handed it to Rita. She studied it for a moment, then held it up in the air. "It looks as if April Sullivan of *Today's World* magazine has won a date with her boss! How about that!"

Tom blinked. April had won a date with him? Hell, April was a newlywed! Why had she even purchased a ticket? Unless, he thought as he eyed the innocent looking, smiling Rita, both raffles were rigged and April was a part of it.

At the moment, he didn't give a damn. At least with April he could spend the evening discussing the magazine.

"Okay, folks." Rita had to raise her voice above the murmurs of disappointment from the women in the crowd. "Let's get on with the show. Go ahead and draw a ticket from the other drum, Mr. Kagan. The next winning ticket will be for dinner with Lili Soulé."

Tom would have sworn that Jules Kagan gritted his teeth at the mention of Lili's name, but he gamely reached into the bin marked HERS, rummaged around for a minute, then finally picked a ticket and held it up.

Rita took the winning raffle ticket with a flourish. She feigned surprise when she announced, "The winner of a dinner date with Lili is none other than Tom Eldridge! Come on up here, Lili. You, too, Tom!"

The audience broke into cheers as a blushing Lili slowly made her way through the crowd to the make-shift stage.

"Your turn, April!" Rita called. "Come on up here!"

Even though Rita had assured him that the odds of winning Lili were in his favor, Tom had been afraid to believe it. Not that he cared what people thought, he mused with a self-conscious grin as he maneuvered through the laughing crowd. The coincidence of two employees on floors eight and nine being the winners surely had to raise suspicion, especially when the raffle had been organized by magazine staffers, but no one seemed to care. He stopped to shake hands, but finally jumped up on the stage.

"I yield my winning ticket to Tom," April called out.

With a soulful thank-you, Tom accepted the winning ticket from Kagan and took Lili's cold hand. She was his again, he thought as he led her off stage. If only for one night.

Chapter Sixteen

Tom glanced at his silent companion as he drove north up Michigan Avenue to the Intercontinental Chicago Hotel. In deference to Lili, he'd chosen the hotel for their raffle date because of its historic charm and stunning blend of furnishings and art from all over the world. If his good intentions and the setting didn't work their magic tonight, he didn't know what would.

Participating in the raffle and convincing Lili to honor the date hadn't been exactly a piece of cake. But not even Kagan's frown when he'd apparently realized the draw was fixed had deterred Tom from taking Lili by the hand and leading her off the stage, amid shouts of encouragement. It was Rita's laughing reminder that fair was fair and that she was a willing baby-sitter that had finally swayed Lili to agree to go out with Tom.

Sometimes a man had to do what he had to do to win the woman he loved.

Off to one side, he'd caught a glimpse of his father making a victory sign. *Dear old dad,* Tom remembered thinking fondly. Maybe his efforts hadn't all been because of grandchildren. Maybe the old man *did* know more about the mating game than his son did.

Tom could only hope that Rita wouldn't fill the twins' fertile minds with some of her wilder ideas.

He handed the hotel parking attendant the car keys, took Lili by the arm and led her inside. When she shivered beside him, he shrugged off his jacket and covered her bare shoulders. Outside of a quiet hello, she hadn't said much since he'd picked her up. Not a good sign, but the night was still young.

The hotel's sweeping four-story lobby featured a grand staircase and impressive cast bronze ornamentation. The walls were lined with beautiful murals.

He led the way across the glittering lobby to the dimly lit dining room, where the low murmur of voices and the scent of flowers filled the air. It was an intimate atmosphere, but Tom didn't intend for the night to end here. He had plans of his own.

The maître d' greeted them with a welcoming smile when Tom identified himself. "Ah yes, Mr. Eldridge. Welcome. We are pleased you have chosen the Intercontinental to help you celebrate this very special occasion. An anniversary?"

When Lili started, Tom drew her close, and pulled her arm through his. "An engagement," he said with a conspiratorial smile at Lili. "As a matter of fact, a very special engagement."

Obviously still reluctant to be here tonight, Lili let Tom draw his jacket off her shoulders. She was wearing a soft blue silk dress that clung to her, and Tom thought she looked more breathtaking than ever.

"I'm not very hungry," she murmured as their waiter led them to a secluded table by the window overlooking glittering Lake Michigan. He handed Tom a wine list.

"In that case, dinner can wait," Tom answered. He gestured to the dance floor, where several couples were slowly revolving to music provided by a string quartet. He didn't hesitate. Dancing was one way to legitimately hold Lili in his arms. "My favorite song," he said as the familiar strains of a tune from the *Phantom of the Opera* flowed through the room. "Shall we dance?" he asked.

After seeing the yearning look in Tom's eyes, Lili couldn't bring herself to say no. Especially when she remembered the last time they'd danced together. With his warm hand on her back, guiding her, she felt as if she was floating. Within moments, she forgot the reason she was here tonight and became the woman she longed to be. A woman in the arms of the man she loved.

The scent of Tom's shaving lotion, the strength of his embrace and his tender smile as he looked down at her sent her into another world. A world where there was no disturbing past, only the present moment.

She closed her eyes and leaned against Tom's solid bulk. "I don't think I've ever really danced before tonight," she said as her heart beat in time to the haunting music.

"Hungry yet?" Tom murmured after a moment. "I see the waiter hovering near our table."

Lili smiled up at him. "Would it be a cliché if I said I feel as if I could dance all night?"

Tom felt as if he could have danced all night, too, but dinner waited. After dinner, his apology. Then, if he could persuade Lili to listen, he would tell her how much he loved her, and show her just how much she meant to him.

He couldn't wait.

"Come on," he finally said, reluctantly letting her go.

"If you're really not hungry, we can eat later. I have another idea."

Even in the dim light on the dance floor, Tom could see Lili blush as she looked up at him questioningly.

"The truth is, I've reserved a room for us upstairs for the night," he murmured. "But only if you're willing. What do you say?"

Lili's blush deepened. After being held in Tom's warm, solid arms, how could she say no? How could she ignore the ache in her heart, the longing to be with him?

If Tom only knew his plan was exactly what she'd been thinking for the past ten minutes.

TOM LET LILI INTO a spacious suite. In the middle of one room there was a small blue-and-white upholstered sofa covered with matching cushions. In another, a king-size bed, whose cobalt-blue and white canopy matched the flowing drapes. She averted her eyes from the bed and wandered to the fireplace, where a low flame glowed. Behind her, Tom called room service.

After their disagreement, she would never have thought to find herself in such an intimate setting with Tom. A man who had planned a pretend engagement largely for his own purposes? A man who appeared to have reservations about her children?

And yet there was something about Tom that had touched her heart in many ways.

It seemed as if only moments later he answered a knock on the door and a waiter rolled a serving cart into the room. There was a bottle of merlot, a silver tray, biscuits, cheese and a plate of fresh fruit.

Lili smiled. The display was inviting, but she intended to first satisfy another hunger.

"A glass of wine?" Tom asked.

Lili nodded. "Please."

His thoughts whirling with ideas on how to reach Lili, Tom poured two glasses of wine and moved to her side. Lili's smile, reflecting the glow from the fireplace, was too lovely to resist. He hesitated, then put the glasses on the coffee table. Drinks could come later. For what he had in mind, he needed both hands.

He reached for Lili. Her eyes remained wary, but he didn't intend to let that stop him. Not now. Not when he had hopes that he and Lili would turn their convenient engagement into one that would become a lifetime commitment.

"Lili, I have something to say and you have to listen to me," he said. "Tell me what I have to do to make you believe I love you?"

"I do believe you," Lili answered, although he heard a hundred doubts in her voice. "But how will you react the next time I do something you disapprove of?"

"We'll talk things over, I promise." Tom massaged her hands as he spoke. "You need to understand there are reasons I've resisted having anyone run my life for me. And," he added with a wry smile, "that largely includes my father and his desire for grandchildren."

At the mention of grandchildren, the expression on Lili's face softened. "I have always believed children are life's dividends," she murmured.

"True," Tom added with a wry smile, "but for a guy like me, getting used to the idea of being a father will take a little time. But that's not why I brought you here. I wanted to explain, to tell you I've never really been in love before as I am now. With you. I can't promise I won't act like a jerk now and again," he added playfully.

"I guess that's part of life, too. If I don't get my act together the first time, you'll just have to show me how to make you happy."

"And the twins?"

"I've never thought that being a father could be fun," Tom answered with a rueful smile. "But I have a feeling it will be with the twins. Although I'm going to have to teach Paulette to kick straight. As for Paul, I'll leave him to Dad. The kid's just as curious about life as my father is. The two ought to make a great pair."

Lili's eyes softened, and a smile teased her lips. "You are sure about this?"

"As sure as I am about loving you," Tom answered as he lifted Lili's hands and kissed them. "If you give me another chance, I'd like to show you how much."

Lili might resist the appeal in Tom's velvet voice, the longing in his eyes. But as his warm lips caressed the back of her hands, bringing a glow to her heart, the last of her reservations faded. She might still be afraid of what the future could bring, but tonight she wanted Tom. She yearned to recapture the magic of being held in his arms, the feel of his body against hers, taking her to a magical place.

Her fears dropped away as she turned into Tom's welcoming embrace and met his searching lips. He tasted of wine and male desire as he kissed her deeply.

"I love you, Lili," he said as he drew her dress off her shoulders. "You belong here in my arms."

"For tonight," she whispered.

"Forever," he corrected with a shaky laugh.

Tom reached behind her to unhook and draw off her bra. He fondled her breasts with gentle hands until she felt mindless with the desire to become his one more time.

Quickly she unbuttoned Tom's shirt and fumbled with the belt of his trousers, then watched with interest as he hurriedly removed the rest of his clothing.

Tom's body was solid and muscular. His skin, as he took her back into his arms, was warm to her touch. The sound of his deep, melodious voice sent desire shooting through her and captured her senses.

She ached to feel more of his skin sliding against hers, his tongue dancing with hers, to watch his eyes light up with the same desire burning inside her. She sank back onto the couch and welcomed him into her arms.

"I love you, Lili," he whispered again as he kissed her in places that ached for his lips. "Love me back?"

Lili's heart responded to the yearning in Tom's voice and the appeal in his eyes as he murmured words of endearment while he kissed her heated body.

She did love Tom, Lili thought as he parted her legs with his and ran his hands over the part of her that longed for him. Tonight, she wanted none of his tenderness. Tonight, she wanted Tom in all the primitive and wild ways a woman wanted a man she wished to make her mate. She pressed down on his heated back and urged him closer.

"I love you back," she whispered, giving him the heart she'd believed he hadn't wanted. He wanted her now, she knew, and her hands closed around the slick, velvety part of him she needed to have inside her.

"Come to me, my Tom," she whispered, straining for that magical moment when she would soar to the skies in his arms.

"Wait for me," Tom gasped as he strained above her, taking her higher and higher into a lovers' universe. "I want to come with you."

When her world burst into hundreds of tiny shining particles, Lili yielded with a sigh, pulled Tom closer and willed the moment to last forever.

Finally, he rolled to one side and gathered her in his arms. "So," he said softly against her lips, "tell me again why we can't make that convenient engagement of ours into a real one?"

Lili slowly came back to reality. She might have forgotten the reason for their estrangement in moments of passion, but she hadn't forgotten Tom's anger at the part she'd played in organizing the contest. Or the fact that she was here only because he had won her in a raffle.

The warm feeling of having been well loved faded.

Under any other circumstances, *would* she have been here tonight?

What of tomorrow?

She leaned back, searching Tom's eyes. "Tell me the truth. I know as well as you that my being here tonight is surely no coincidence. How *did* you manage to have the winning ticket?"

Tom swore softly under his breath. He should have known Lili was too perceptive to have believed he'd won her as his date purely by chance.

It was time for the truth.

"I'm sure it took some doing," he said, "but I swear I wasn't in on Rita's schemes. All I did was buy a hundred raffle tickets and pray." He reached for Lili and uttered another prayer that her natural curiosity would carry them through the next few moments without heartbreak.

"Come on back here and I'll tell you everything I *do* know," he added when she was silent. "You'll have to promise not to be angry. The truth is that everything that happened in the raffle caper, honest or not, is only because there are a number of people who care for you. That includes me."

Lili didn't look convinced.

Tom smiled reassuringly into her eyes. "It all began this way." He ran his fingers over her bare shoulders, still damp from their lovemaking, and kissed a drop of moisture from her forehead. "Like I said, I was asked to buy a hundred raffle tickets with the chance I might hold the winning ticket. To tell the truth, when I considered the number of tickets that might be sold, I was dubious at first about my chances of winning. Then I realized I was being made an offer I couldn't refuse. Even if I didn't win you, I knew that the thousand dollars would go for a good cause."

Lili stirred as he smoothed away the furrow on her forehead with loving fingers. "That is all?"

"That's the truth, I swear. But as long as we're talking about the contest, you'll be happy to know that I hear Jules Kagan has agreed to match all the money you've managed to raise."

Lili looked amazed. "You are sure?"

"Yes, after my father softened him up," Tom admitted with a grin. "Dad managed to come up with that idea as a sort of compromise so the guy could save face. Although how Dad persuaded him to participate in the raffle draw beats me. Whatever he said worked. So in return," Tom added as he tugged Lili around to face him, "I guess I'll have to forgive my father."

"For changing Mr. Kagan's mind?"

"No," Tom said, as he went back to his task of loving Lili, "for helping make me realize how much I love you."

Lili's reply was to push him back onto the couch and lean over him again. "Show me."

Tom grinned happily as he gazed up into Lili's sparking eyes. "Again?"

"Yes," she said, suddenly serious, "but first I have a confession of my own to make."

Tom swept her silken hair away from her damp forehead. "Confess away, but make it quick. We have some unfinished business to take care of."

Remembering the old adage that confession was good for the soul, Lili took a deep breath. "What happened between us was just as much my fault as yours. I should have trusted you. I'm afraid I need to curb some of my impulsive ways."

Tom put his fingers over her lips. "Don't ever change, my darling Lili. I love you just the way you are. Although," he added with mock seriousness, "there *is* one change I'd like to make."

Lili blinked, but just as she felt confession was good for the soul, she realized that only an act of contrition could clear her conscience. "What is this change?"

"Marry me?"

Her heart was full as she realized the depth of the commitment Tom was making. And how difficult it must have been for him to make it. As for herself, their coming together made her feel as if she'd come home again.

"Umm," Lili purred with a wicked smile. "Kiss me some more."

"I take it that's a yes?" Tom said between kisses.

"We will marry, yes," she answered as Tom held her to him and made her his once more.

And this time, Tom realized he'd actually captured

Lili's smile in his portrait of her. The smile was the smile of a woman who knew she was loved.

All that was left now was to make Lili happy. And to do that, all he had to do was love her.

* * * * *

Welcome to the world of American Romance!
Turn the page for excerpts from
our July 2005 titles.

A SOLDIER'S RETURN
by Judy Christenberry

TEMPORARY DAD
by Laura Marie Altom

THE BABY SCHEME
by Jacqueline Diamond

A TEXAS STATE OF MIND
by Ann DeFee

We hope you enjoy every one of these books!

Bestselling author and reader favorite Judy Christenberry delivers another emotion-filled family drama from her Children of Texas miniseries, with *A Soldier's Return*. Witness a touching reunion when the Barlow sisters meet their long-lost older brother, and find out how the heart of this brooding warrior is healed by an impressible beauty—an extended member of his rediscovered family.

Carrie Abrams was working on her computer when she heard the door of the detective agency open.

She turned her body to greet the entrant, but her head was still glued to the computer screen. When she reluctantly brought her gaze to focus on the tall man with straight posture standing by the door wearing a dress uniform, she gasped.

"Jim! I mean, uh, sorry, I mistook you for someone I—um, may I help you?" She abandoned her clumsy beginning and became as stiff as he was.

"I need to speak with Will Greenfield."

"And your name?" She almost held her breath.

"Captain James Barlow."

"Thank you, Captain Barlow. Just one moment, please."

She got up from her desk, wishing she'd worn a business suit instead of jeans. You're being silly. Jim Barlow wouldn't care what she was wearing. He didn't even know her.

She rapped on Will's door, opened it and stepped inside.

"He's here!" She whispered so the man in the outer office wouldn't hear her.

"Who—" Will started to ask, but Carrie didn't wait.

"Jim! He's here. He's wearing his uniform. He wants to speak to you."

Will's face broke into a smile. "Well, show him in!"

Carrie opened the door. "Captain Barlow, please come in."

She wanted to stay in Will's office, but she knew he wouldn't extend the invitation. And she wouldn't ask. It wouldn't be professional.

As she leaned against the door, reluctant to break contact with the two men inside, her gaze roamed her desk.

"Oh, no!" she gasped, and rushed forward. Jim's picture. Had he seen it? She hoped not. How could she explain her fascination with Vanessa's oldest brother? She'd been enthralled by his square-jawed image, just as Vanessa had been. He was the picture of protective, strong…safe. The big brother every little girl dreamed of.

Her best friend, Vanessa Shaw, had probably dreamed those dreams while being raised as an only child. Then, after her father's death, her mother had told her she had five siblings. That revelation had set in motion a lot of changes in their lives.

Carrie drew a deep breath. It was so tempting to call Vanessa and break the news. But she couldn't do that. That was Will's privilege.

All she could do was sit here and pretend indifference that Jim Barlow had returned to the bosom of his family after twenty-three years.

Temporary Dad is the kind of story American Romance readers love—with moments that will make you laugh (and a moment now and then that'll bring you to tears). Jed Hale is an all-American hero: a fireman, a rescuer, a family man. And Annie Harris is just the woman for him. Join these two on their road trip from Oklahoma to Colorado, with three babies in tow (his triplet niece and nephews, temporarily in his care). Enjoy their various roadside stops—like the Beer Can Cow and the Giant Corncob. And smile as they fall in love....

Waaaaaaaaaaaaaaa! Waa huh waaaaaaaaaAAAHH!

From a cozy rattan chair on the patio of her new condo, Annie Harris looked up from the August issue of Budget Decorating and frowned.

Waaaaaaaaaaa!

Granted, she wasn't yet a mother herself, but she had been a preschool teacher for the past seven years, so that did lend her a certain credibility where children were concerned.

WAAAAA HA waaaaaaa!

Annie sighed.

She thought whoever was in charge of that poor, pitiful wailer in the condo across the breezeway from hers ought to try something to calm the infant. Never had she heard so much commotion. Was the poor thing sick?

WAAAAAAAAA WAAAAAAA WAAAAAAA!

WAAAAAAA Huh WAAAAA!

WAAAAAAAAAAA!

Annie slapped the magazine back to her knees.

Something about the sound of that baby wasn't right.

Was there more than one?

Definitely two.

Maybe even three.

But she'd moved in a couple weeks earlier and hadn't heard a peep or seen signs of any infant in the complex—let alone three—which was partially why she'd chosen this unit over the one beside the river that had had much better views of the town of Pecan, Oklahoma.

WAAAAAA Huh WAAAAAAAAA!

Again Annie frowned.

No good parent would just leave an infant to cry like this. Could something else be going on? Could the baby's mom or dad be hurt?

Annie popped the latch on her patio gate, creeping across grass not quite green or brown, but a weary shade somewhere in between.

WAAAAAAAAAAA!

She crept farther across the shared lawn, stepping onto the weathered brick breezeway she shared with the as-yet-unseen owner of the unit across from hers.

The clubhouse manager—Veronica, a bubbly redhead with a penchant for eighties rock and yogurt—said a bachelor fireman lived there.

Judging by the dead azalea bushes on either side of

his front door, Annie hoped the guy was better at watering burning buildings than poor, thirsty plants!

Waaaaaa Huhhhh WAAAAA!

She looked at the fireman's door, then her own.

Whatever was going on inside his home probably wasn't any of her business.

WaaaaaAAAAA!

Call her a busybody, but enough was enough.

She just couldn't bear standing around listening to a helpless baby—maybe even more than one helpless baby—cry.

Her first knock on the bachelor fireman's door was gentle. Ladylike. That of a concerned neighbor.

When that didn't work, she gave the door a few good, hard thuds.

She was just about to investigate the French doors on the patio that matched her own when the forest-green front door flew open—"Patti? Where the?— Oh, sorry. Thought you were my sister."

Annie gaped.

What else could she do faced with the handsomest man she'd ever seen hugging not one baby, not two babies, but three?

Like Alli Gardner, the heroine of The Baby Scheme, Jacqueline Diamond knows about newspapers. She worked as an Associated Press reporter for many years. You'll love this story of a woman who puts her investigative talents to the test—together with a very attractive private investigator—as the two try to unravel a blackmail scheme targeting parents who've adopted babies from a Central American orphanage.

"I'm here about the story in this morning's paper," Alli said to her managing editor. "The one concerning Mayor LeMott."

"Ned tells me you were working on something similar." J.J. eased into his seat. "He says Payne warned him you might have a complaint."

"It wasn't similar. This is my story," Alli told him. "Word for word."

"But you hadn't filed it yet."

"I'd written it but I was holding off so I could double-check a couple of points," she explained. "And there's a sidebar I didn't have time to complete. Mr. Morosco, Payne's planted spyware in my laptop. He stole every bit of that from me."

The editor's forehead wrinkled. He'd been working such long hours he'd begun to lose his tan and had put on a few pounds, she noted. "The two of you have never gotten along, have you? He'd only been here a month when you accused him of stealing your notebook."

"It disappeared from my desk right after he passed by, and the next day he turned in a story based on my research!"

"A guard found your notebook outside that afternoon, right next to where you usually park," the M.E. said.

"I didn't drop it. I'm not that careless." Alli hated being put on the defensive. "Look, you can talk to any of the people I quoted in today's story and they'll confirm who did the reporting."

"Except that most of your sources spoke anonymously," he pointed out.

"I was going to identify them to Ned when I handed it in!" That was standard procedure. "Besides, since when does this paper assign two people to the same story?"

She'd heard of a few big papers that ran their operations in such a cutthroat manner, but the Outlook couldn't afford such a waste of staff time. Besides, that kind of competition did horrible things to morale.

"He says Payne asked if he could pursue the same subject. He decided to let the kid show what he could do, and he beat you to the punch."

How could she win when the assistant managing editor was stabbing her in the back? If she were in J.J.'s seat, she probably wouldn't believe her, either.

"Give Payne his own assignment, something he can't steal from anyone else," she said. "He'll blow it."

"As it happens, he's going to have plenty of chances." J.J. fiddled with some papers. "I'm sure you're aware that I've streamlined two other sections. In the meantime, the publisher and Ned and I have been tossing around ideas for the news operation. I'm about to put those proposals into effect."

Why was he telling her this? Allie wondered uneasily. And why was he avoiding her gaze?

"The publisher believes we've got too much duplication and dead wood," he went on. "Some of the older staff members will be asked to take early retirement, but I'm going to have to cut deeper. After careful consideration, I'm afraid we have to let you go."

American Romance is delighted to introduce a brand-new author. You'll love Ann DeFee's sassy humor, her high-energy writing and her really entertaining characters. She'll make you laugh—and occasionally gasp. And she'll take you to a Texas town you'll never want to leave. (Fortunately you can visit Port Serenity again next June!)

Oooh, boy! Lolly raised her Pepsi in a tribute to Meg Ryan. Could that girl fake the big O! Lord knows Lolly had perfected the very same skill before Wendell, her ex, hightailed it out to Las Vegas to find fame and fortune as a drummer. Good old Wendell—more frog than prince. But to give credit where credit was due, he had managed to sire two of the most fantastic kids in the world.

Nowadays she didn't have to worry about Wendell's flagging ego or, for that matter, any of his other wilting body parts. Celibacy had some rewards—not many, but a few.

Meg had just segued from the throes of parodied passion to a big smile when Lolly's cell phone rang.

"Great, just great," Lolly muttered. She thumped her Pepsi on the coffee table.

"Chief, I hate to call you right at supper time, but I figured you'd want to handle this one. I just got a call from Bud out at the Peaceful Cove Inn, and he's got hisself something of a problem." An after-hours call from the Port Serenity Police Department's gravel-voiced night dispatcher signaled the end to her evening of popcorn and chick flicks.

Chief of police Lavinia "Lolly" Lee Hamilton La-Tullipe sighed. Her hectic life as a single mom and head of a small police force left her with very little free time, and when she had a few moments, she wanted to spend them at home with Amanda and Bren, not out corralling scumbags.

"Cletus is on duty tonight, and that man can handle anything short of a full-scale riot," Lolly argued, even though she knew her objections were futile.

Lordy. She'd rather eat Aunt Sissy's fruitcake than abandon the comfort of her living room, especially when Meg was about to find Mr. Right. Lolly hadn't even been able to find Mr. Sorta-Right, though she'd given it the good old college try. Wendell looked pretty good on the outside, but inside he was like an overripe watermelon—mushy and tasteless. Too bad she hadn't noticed that shortcoming when they started dating in high school. Back then his antics were cute; at thirty-seven they weren't quite so appealing.

"I'd really rather not go out tonight."

"Yes, ma'am. I understand. But this one involves Precious." The dispatcher chuckled when Lolly groaned.

Precious was anything but precious. She was the

seventeen-year-old demon daughter of Mayor Lance Barton, Lolly's boss and a total klutz in the single-dad department. She and Lance had been buddies since kindergarten, so without a doubt she'd be making an unwanted trip to the Peaceful Cove Inn.

"Oh, man. What did I do to deserve that brat in my life?" Lolly rubbed her forehead in a vain attempt to ward off the headache she knew was coming. "Okay, what's she done now?"

"Seems she's out there with some guys Bud don't know, and she's got a snoot full. He figured we'd want to get her home before someone saw her."

Lolly sighed. "All right, I'll run out and see what I can do. Call her daddy and tell him what's happening."

She muttered an expletive as she marched to the rolltop desk in the kitchen to retrieve her bag, almost tripping over Harvey, the family's gigantic mutt. She strapped on an ankle holster and then checked her Taser and handcuffs. In this business, a girl had to be prepared.

Amanda, her ten-year-old daughter, was immersed in homework, and as usual, her fourteen-year-old son had his head poked inside the refrigerator.

"Bren, get Amanda to help you with the kitchen." Lolly stopped him as he tried to sneak out of the room and nodded at the open dishwasher and pile of dishes in the sink. "I've got to go out for a few minutes. If you need anything call Mee Maw."

Her firstborn rolled his eyes. "Aw, Mom."

Lolly suppressed the urge to laugh, and instead employed the dreaded raised eyebrow. The kid was in dire need of a positive male role model. Someone stable, upright, respectable and…safe. Yeah, safe. It was time to find a nice, reliable prince—an orthodontist might be good, considering Amanda's overbite.

"I'm leaving. You guys be good," Lolly called out as she opened the screen door.

HARLEQUIN®

AMERICAN *Romance®*

Fatherhood

Fatherhood: what really defines a man.

It's the one thing all women admire in a man—
a willingness to be responsible for a child and
to care for that child with tenderness and love.

**Meet two men who are true fathers
in every sense of the word!**

Eric Norvald is devoted to his seven-year-old
daughter, Phoebe. But can he give her what she
really wants—a mommy? Find out in

Pamela Browning's
THE MOMMY WISH (AR #1070)

Available June 2005.

In

Laura Marie Altom's
TEMPORARY DAD (AR #1074),

Annie Harnesberry has sworn off men—especially
single fathers. But when her neighbor—a gorgeous
male—needs help with his triplet five-month-old
niece and nephews, Annie can't resist offering
her assistance.

Available July 2005.

If you enjoyed what you just read,
then we've got an offer you can't resist!

Take 2 bestselling love stories FREE!

Plus get a FREE surprise gift!

HARLEQUIN *Super* ROMANCE®

BLACKBERRY HILL MEMORIAL

Almost A Family
by **Roxanne Rustand**
Harlequin Superromance #1284

From Roxanne Rustand,
author of *Operation: Second Chance*
and *Christmas at Shadow Creek*,
a new heartwarming miniseries,
set in a small-town hospital,
where people come first.

As long as the infamous Dr. Connor Reynolds stays
out of her way, Erin has more pressing issues to
worry about. Like how to make her adopted children
feel safe and loved after her husband walked out on
them, and why patients keep dying for no apparent
reason. If only she didn't need Connor's help. And if
only he wasn't so good to her and the kids.

Available July 2005 wherever Harlequin books are sold.

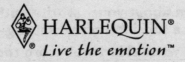

HARLEQUIN®
Live the emotion™

www.eHarlequin.com   HSRAAF0605

AMERICAN *Romance*®

is thrilled to bring you
a heartwarming miniseries
by bestselling author

Judy Christenberry

Separated during childhood, three beautiful
sisters from the Lone Star state are destined
to rediscover one another, find true love and
build a Texas-sized family legacy they can
call their own....

You won't want to miss the third installment
of this beloved family saga!

A SOLDIER'S RETURN

(HAR #1073)

On sale July 2005.

AMERICAN *Romance*®

**The bigger the family, the greater the love—
and the more people trying to ruin your life!**

A TEXAS STATE OF MIND
by Ann DeFee
(HAR #1076)

Single mother of two Lavinia "Lolly" LaTullipe
has plenty to do as police chief of the little
Texas town of Port Serenity. But her job
becomes even more complicated when
Christian Delacroix, an undercover DEA cop,
comes to town to help solve a case. When he
and Lolly meet, the sparks fly—literally!

Available July 2005.